A Touch of

Love

Bob Richey

Published by:

Book Cover by Zsa Zsa   Paperback

Illustrations by Zsa Zsa

ISBN: 978-1-970990-00-3
5-
Second edition 2025

DEDICATED TO YOU

This book is dedicated to you, the person reading this message. I am old now and this story has been on my bucket list for the last 20 years. But it is not finished. This story started as a movie script. Although I've watched this movie numerous times in my mind, I would really like to watch it on the big screen. Perhaps with your help, that could become a reality.

A Touch of Love

The Story of a man's quest to find his past,

and a young woman's search for her future.

Written by: Bob Richey

Based on a story originally discussed by: Bob Richey

Ross Abplanalp

Andy Caley

Bill Shoemaker

ii

A Touch of Love

Preface

From what realm does an idea manifest? The spark for an idea, usually comes from a realization after something has been experienced. After a dream, a conversation, a happening or any other human experience, an idea can spring to life.

My question back in 2007, was can we brainstorm an idea for a movie? The project, originally named "Feeling Lonely" came to life in a meeting of Ross Abplanalp, Andy Caley, Bill Shumaker and myself. We convened four meetings, complete with binders and clipboards. The four of us worked out a story of a lonely computer repairman.

I should interject here, that the compelling reason for these meetings, was the absence of Matt McDaniel. Matt had been making short amusing movies with the aforementioned. His return to Seattle after university, and the formation of his photography business caused a longing in the guys to find a way to continue without him.

iii

Although we never concocted a story, the groundwork and the storyline was widely discussed. Time has dulled everyone's memories, but I believe we had carved out a good part of what has become the first chapter. They would know better than me, as I kept the story alive in my head long after the meetings stopped and the others lost interest.

I obsessed the story in my head. It consumed my thoughts and imagination. The story was always running in the back of my head as I went about my life. It didn't quit until I finished watching the movie in my head and I was overcome with a deep satisfaction. It was a good movie. I tried to tell Ross, then Andy. Neither showed interest. Both were polite and allowed me to tell my story, but neither lasted to the ending. It's a long story and a short novel. Over the years, I've wrote some of the story down, replaying it in my mind. I continued my writing a dozen times, each time remembering and enhancing the story. After I survived Covid, I got serious and got to the one-third mark or so. I put what I had written so far on the web and waited for someone to read it and realize it wasn't finished. I thought I would be inspired to tell the story if someone else was interested. That never happened.

I'm old now and I felt a need to tie up some loose ends in my life. This story was one of them. My caregiver Juliana, not only started doing most of my daily chores, giving me free time, she also encouraged me to write the rest. She read the story off the website out loud to me, knowing it wasn't finished. While she read, I replayed the movie in my mind, reminding me of the parts I had written and refreshing the rest of the book in my head. She was instrumental in me finishing of this book. She has said that she really likes it, but that's what she would say no matter what. Please read the story and inform me as to whether she was telling me the truth or not.

A Touch of Love

Chapter 1

It All Started in the Desert

Joe wasn't normal. He wasn't normal and he knew it. It wasn't something you could put your finger on, nor was it something a stranger might see from a distance. He had always been that way, or for at least as long as he could remember. Looking at the meat counter, he picked up a rib eye steak and examined the price. It was marked $34.99, and he quickly put it back, choosing a package of hamburger instead. As he moved on to find some bread, he thought about just that. He wondered what had happened that put him in this spot; not just this spot in the Safeway supermarket, but everything about him. Ever since that day he wandered out of the desert dazed and confused, Joe tried hard to remember a time before this and wondered what might have happened. He thought about that day as he picked out some hamburger buns.

He was lucky; he wasn't injured in any way, just thirsty and hungry and tired, so very tired. A traveler had seen him stumble and stopped, backing his car to pick him up. They stopped at a roadside diner, and the stranger marveled at Joe, watching him drink glass after glass of water. After a quick sandwich, they drove on, and at the outskirts of the next town, he dropped Joe off and proceeded into town.

A whole series of events one would call lucky started to happen. A sign on the road said "Recycling Yard." As Joe walked towards the driveway to it, he saw two good-sized trees and an old couch just before the fence. He rolled the couch over and positioned it under the trees. The gate was locked, and someone had recently just thrown the couch off and left. He was asleep before he knew he had laid down.

"Are you buying that?" the cashier said.

"Oh, sorry, umm, yeah," he said.

"Just when are you going to get a card like everybody else?" she said as he handed her the money.

"Soon, soon," he said. "Just when are you going to tell me you won't take cash?"

"Soon, soon," she replied, and they both chuckled.

Joe walked home. He didn't own a car or even a driver's license. He couldn't. He really didn't have a name or a home. He took the name Joe Smith in an effort to be discreet. He didn't want to stand out or be noticeably different until he found out what his past was like. That's been over three years now. As far as home goes, well, he lives in an office in the building he rents. He rents the space to run a small computer repair business. The owner of the building is not very friendly but doesn't really care what goes on as long as he's paid, on time and in cash. So, he works, eats, and sleeps in a little town called Hope, always working on learning who he is and where he's from.

Tum, tump, thump, "Not now!" Diane said out loud. Tum, tump, thump, the car answered as she drove to work. Quietly, she turned around and headed to the local garage. Tum, tump, THUMP! As she turned in, she thought, they must have heard that!

A Touch of Love

While waiting in line, the mechanic that had looked at the car before came up and asked, "Is it making that noise again?"

"Yes," she said.

"Well, let's go for a ride," he said as he smiled at her.

He liked her and she knew it, but how could someone always be so dirty, she thought? She drove around the block thinking; the smell of the oil and grease won't wash off easy either.

He listened as she drove and politely said, "Do you hear the noise?"

"NO!" she said sternly. "It's a loud noise! You will hear it very clearly and loud!"

"Okay," he said, "but I don't hear a noise."

Diane went around again, faster this time. She jammed on the brakes then sped up.

She swerved and swore, but nothing would make the car make the noise.

"It's hopeless," she said. "It just won't make the damn noise anytime you are in the car!"

"Maybe it fixed itself," the mechanic told her. "Sometimes," he explained, "things just seem to fix themselves. I had a TV that wouldn't turn on once. When the repairman came, it turned right on. Cost me fifty bucks, but I know the darn thing just fixed itself. You're lucky, I'm not going to charge you anything," he finished. "The darn thing just fixed itself."

She couldn't get that out of her head as she drove quietly back towards work. Hmm, she thought, he was kind of cute and nice too, but the odor of gasoline was lingering in her car.

"So, you fixed yourself, can you do something about this smell?" she mumbled to the car.

A Touch of Love

Honk! Honk! The horn woke him off the couch with a start!

"You can't sleep there!" a man in a convertible yelled.

The gates rumbled open and he drove in. Pleased that there was no penalty or inquisition, Joe grabbed a hold of the couch and dragged it into the facility.

"If you're gonna drag that in here, put it over there by the furniture," said the man in the car while pointing.

Joe picked the whole couch up into the air and carried it over to the other furniture.

"You're strong, and you need a place to sleep. I'll bet you need a job, too! I'm Jim Thompson. Call me Jimbo, everybody does. This is my place here, my junk, my stuff. People drop it off, discard it, or sell it really cheap, and if it has any value, I resell it; if it doesn't, we break it down to recycle the copper and aluminum and, well, you know the drill, right?"

When Jimbo finished his speech, Joe nodded and said, "Right, and I, uh, I need that job, too."

"Then it's settled," Jimbo shrieked. "There's a cot in the back room you can sleep on until you get on your feet. There is a hotplate back there, a coffee pot too."

"Thank you very much," Joe replied. "Thank you, thank you, you won't regret this." So now with a job and a place to sleep, Joe's lucky streak continued.

Joe carried the groceries as he walked to his computer repair shop. Joe's appearance, gait, and aura all pointed to the fact that he was lonely. Sure, the business was going well and his customers came and left all day, giving him brief periods of dialogue, but he didn't have any real friends or relationships other than Jimbo. The shop was not anything at all like working for Jimbo. Over the years of working at the recycling center, or dump as some called it, Joe and Jimbo had become good friends. Jimbo had a gigantic personality and was very outgoing, often bringing stories on Monday of his weekend conquests. Jimbo was popular, very popular. Important people from the town visited the center often, usually buying something from the warehouse that Joe had recovered and repaired. Jimbo was friendly and Joe's best friend, maybe because he too had his quirks. The worst was his constant effort not to touch anything. He wore two pairs of gloves, one on top of the other. If he saw something in the pile, he would have Joe get it and bring it to him; he never went out and rummaged as someone in that business was likely to do. He washed his hands often, and, well, he washed his hands with his gloves still on. He would then take them off, wash his hands and put clean gloves on, two pairs. Joe never mentioned the gloves and stuff, and Jimbo never mentioned the odd behavior of Joe. It worked out to a pretty good friendship.

As he reached the store, he unlocked the door and put the groceries on the counter. He then went back to the door and flipped the open and closed sign to show "open."

Chapter 2

Cash only

Diane pulled her car into the parking garage and parked near an exit. She checked her makeup and reapplied her perfume. A great mixture of gas, oil and Chanel No. 5, she thought. She would walk the two blocks to the van. Click, click, click, her high heels echoed in the ramp. As she turned onto the sidewalk, it was apparent that she was somewhat overdressed for this part of town. It wasn't a bad section of Hope; there were no bad sections in Hope. It just wasn't the downtown area where she would fit in better. She really didn't care. She dressed professionally. She dressed overly professionally. She looked great and she knew it. No more of the jeans and sweatshirts that she was recommended to wear. No, she had been passed up on too many of the recent promotions, simply for blending in too well. I'm done sitting in that stuffy van with Kurt all day, it's time for a change, she thought. She casually looked around as she approached the van, then opened the door, looked over her shoulder and stepped up into the dark space. It was lit only by the many LCD lights on the equipment.

"Late again," Kurt said as she settled into her seat. "Let me guess? The car was making that noise again, right?" Kurt wasn't really upset with her being late. He was right at home in this mess of technology. "I told you to bring it over to my place some weekend and I'd take a look at it," he reminded her. He didn't seem to notice or care that she was ignoring him.

"Geez, Kurt, what are you looking at with my equipment?" she squawked back, changing the subject. "Wait, you were watching me the whole way from the garage? What the hell?"

"Gotta keep an eye on my partner," he offered.

"Just leave my station alone," she demanded. "This will take me all morning to get back straightened out."

"I'll help you," he said.

"No," she quickly replied.

The rest of the morning was spent quietly as Diane reoriented all her equipment while Kurt probably scanned the area for anything of interest. This work was all taking place in a common looking white van that said Hope Restaurant Supplies on the side. The large camera lens was almost undetectable, hidden in the 'o' in Hope.

A Touch of Love

It was a quiet morning; actually, dead quiet, as not one customer had stopped to either pick up or drop off a computer. Joe finished his hamburger and was just getting ready to put the open sign out again when a burly guy with orange suspenders and a yellow hardhat banged on the door. "Coming," he said, and in one motion both opened the door and flipped the sign.

"I gotta get this fixed real fast," he said. "I need this for work."

"Sure," said Joe, "but I don't fix computers for businesses. I just work on personal computers and everything is paid in cash," he stated as he pointed to a big sign that said CASH ONLY.

"No problem," said the construction worker. "This is mine and I'll pay! I put all my work papers on this laptop and I shouldn't have." He continued, somewhat frantic, "I need this to start! I need to get it working and get back to work. Can you help?"

"I will certainly try," Joe replied, and he took the laptop and disappeared into a back room. The worker paced back and forth, while Joe, amid six or seven laptops and computer towers on the table, made room and set it down.

Joe opened the laptop and pushed the button. Whirr, click, click, beep, the machine came to life. The screen lit brightly and everything seemed to work just fine. Joe checked the mouse and inspected the cover. He wiped it down and restarted it. It started again just fine. He picked up the laptop, still running, and returned to the counter.

"Just a loose wire," Joe lied. "Could be more, but I figured you were in a hurry. See, it's working just fine now."

The man in the bright yellow hard hat was wide-eyed and seemed amazed. "You saved my life, man! You don't know how glad I am! This is great! What do I owe you?"

"Forty dollars," Joe said. "Cash, you know."

"Great, here! Keep the change," he said as he scooped up the laptop and took it back outside. Once outside he quickly wheeled around and went back in. "Wait," he said, "I mean it when I say thanks!" He stretched out his arm and big grizzled hand and said, "You really saved the day." They shook hands and he left again.

Joe sat there quietly thinking. He was happy, the customer was happy, the laptop is working, and it fixed itself, what's wrong with that?

Diane watched as a man in a bright yellow hat hurriedly walked down the street and into the store. She saw Joe greet him at the door and wondered if this was the rent payoff they were watching for. No, this wasn't how someone in an underworld crime ring would dress. Then she thought about how she wasn't dressed like her boss expected her to dress. Nah, she thought, this guy is probably just working down the road on the road construction. She paid close attention as he was in there and noted that he seemed quite happy as he left. She looked up and Kurt was watching too. Good, she thought, he's finally doing something he's supposed to be doing.

People came and left the rest of the day and nothing of note happened. As they were packing up for the day, Kurt made the offhand comment that it's a wonder he stays in business with all the unhappy customers.

She just smiled at him and said, "Well, the guy in the yellow hat was sure happy!"

"That guy?" Kurt didn't want to argue as he thought, she smiled at me, and she's into me, I'm sure. All Diane thought was, what an idiot, as she walked to her car.

Joe closed the shop and went into the back room. He sat down surrounded by the computers that had been dropped off the past few days. He opened and turned on a laptop, and as it was starting, continued to start computer after computer. Each one whirred and beeped as it started. They were all fixed just fine as he expected. He hit restart on each one to be sure, and after a bit, turned them all off and started calling their owners. "Fifty dollars," he would say, "corrupted programs," or "virus infestation." Sometimes he used the old reliable, "loose wire." He would always end the call saying, "Low charges and cash only."

Joe didn't feel bad or awkward anymore for charging customers and not really having to do anything to fix their items. He had gotten over that at Jimbo's. At the recycling yard, he had rescued many things that were broken and discarded. In fact, many of the things in the office had been cleaned up and repaired, ready for reuse. He went in the office and used the repaired hotplate to cook up the hamburger. It works just fine, he thought. It wouldn't make any sense to throw it away; this old hotplate still has some value left in it. Why shouldn't it be resold to someone that can take advantage of a low price? The computers that I fix would likely just end up at the dump anyway. I'm just skipping a step and making people happy, so why wouldn't helping things along to fix themselves be worth something? I'm just lucky!

Being lucky is how Joe met Walter, Jimbo's brother and now his landlord. Jimbo had been praising Joe to Walter and after saying Joe was exceptionally lucky, Jimbo proposed that all three pick out an item from the heap and see if their pick worked or not. Jimbo put on yet another pair of gloves and they walked down the stairs from the landing dock.

"Here," Jimbo said, "I'll pick this radio."

"I'll play along," Walter said, as he picked up an interesting item unaware of what it was.

"That's a wireless router," said Joe. "It connects you to the Internet." Joe rummaged around and dug out an organ-like keyboard that actually didn't look half bad. They each carried their item up to that loading dock and sat them on a big table.

"I'll plug this radio in," Jimbo said, and immediately started fiddling with the knobs and buttons. "Nothing!" he cried. "Not even a light, I knew it! Let's check yours, Walter." Walter plugged in the little router and everyone waited, but nothing, not even a light on it either. Walter picked the router up and wham,

wham, wham, slammed it down onto the desk three times, but still nothing.

"We're waiting!" they both said in unison, looking directly at Joe. Joe plugged the keyboard in and a fan quietly whirred. They all heard the fan and watched silently as the light blinked on and off and then settled with three LEDs each glowing green.

"Well, try it, Joe!" Jimbo exclaimed with a big smile. "Show off some of your lucky to Walter." Joe touched a few keys, bon, boom, bah... the keyboard came to life. He pushed a button on the top and boom, bah, pa, boom, bah, pa, a drum beat continued playing. Another button pressed started a horn section, and the touch of a few keys soon had a beautiful little song playing just about as good as you could hope for.

"Looks like it works just fine, guys," Joe said. "A little polish and it's worth about a hundred bucks."

"What did I tell you!" Jimbo exclaimed as he did something that he rarely did. Jimbo smacked his cousin Walt right in the middle of his back. "I told you he was lucky; I knew he would win. I knew it would work."

Walter looked at him with a scowl, but as he turned to Joe it changed to a slight smile. "Good one," he said. "That was fun. Jimbo was right, you're okay, you ever need some help, you come find me, maybe even fix something for me, and I'll treat you right." That day came sooner than later.

She unlocked the door and on the way to the kitchen kicked off one shoe then the other. She wasn't physically tired; it was a mental tiredness she was fighting as she slid to a stop at the counter. She grabbed an already open bottle of wine and a glass before retiring to her comfy chair. She put her feet up and realized how good it felt while massaging her feet with each other. Those heels better pay off, she thought. She sat there sipping her wine and reluctantly reached over for her laptop to check her email.

"Damn it!" she said out loud. The very first email was from her boss about a meeting with her in the morning. "On Friday? Why can't we have these meetings on Monday? Everyone already hates to go in on Monday. This will surely ruin my whole weekend." That really wasn't possible though; Diane's weekend was a blank. She didn't have anything planned with anybody. She didn't even have a dog or a cat to keep her company. She didn't lament about being lonely. No, she would just end up sitting in her comfy chair all weekend reading romance novels, like she did last weekend and the weekend before that. Oh well, a ruined

A Touch of Love

weekend is one thing, but Kurt is going to be all up in me saying I'm late again, damn, he'll mess with my stuff again and I'll be all afternoon getting things set up, only to tear everything back down for the weekend.

Chapter 3

Internal Revenue Service

Diane's alarm went off early, too early. She got up quickly, shook off her wine-induced sleep and hurried to the shower. As she showered, she contemplated how to dress. I am just not going to follow those instructions to dress plain so to blend in, she thought. The main office is going to notice me when I go in and I'm the one they're going to be gossiping about, for today at least.

She put on her makeup and then the dress. She was wearing the dress she had bought for a dinner party that had been canceled at the last minute because of an illness. It had hung right there in plain sight, waiting for an occasion, and this was just the occasion Diane had planned. She playfully looked into the mirror and tried to pose, "I got this," she whispered. The hour-long drive back to the city gave her time to daydream. I want your job, she imagined saying to her boss. Not that she would, or even wanted her boss's job, no, she wanted any promotion that would get her into the office. She desperately wanted out of the field and out of that dark, dank van with Kurt. She wanted to feel the pulse of the office, department and especially the city. In the field she was alone and cut off from everyone except Kurt. The drive was uneventful until the noise. Tum, tump, THUMP! Diane listened, Tum, tump, THUMP! Oh, not now! she thought. "Okay fine," she said aloud, "either break or fix yourself!" The rest of the ride was quiet and she soon returned to her thoughts. When she arrived at the tall glass and metal building, she parked and as she got out of the car, paused and looked at the big sign that read Internal Revenue Service, then put her head in both hands and mouthed, "I hope this goes well."

Late again, Kurt thought. He finished starting his machines and shifted into her seat. Swinging the camera around, he zoomed in, one block then another all the way to the parking garage. Nothing yet, he thought. She really didn't have to be here early like Kurt. He got all the wheels turning and brought the inside of the van to life. He understood the technical parts of the spy and recording hardware and software. He could keep things hidden and running smoothly. Diane's job was more to keep things focused on the important areas and to cut out all the unnecessary and boring mundane footage and splice together the important parts to make prosecution possible. The department had a motto, "We Use Evidence and Only Evidence," and Diane was quite good at trimming the fat off all the tapes and only presenting the important evidence. Kurt continued to check for Diane to be coming as he recorded a rather busy day for the store. Sometimes watching and sometimes not, people came and went without any real indication of anything afoul. Lunch came and went without incident but Kurt was checking for Diane more and more often.

Joe closed the shop for lunch. He just went through the motions to close, because if someone came by and knocked, he would let them right in and most of his regular customers knew that. He went into the back and positioned the new computers that were dropped off, two laptops and a PlayStation. Joe was comfortable here in the back. He was surrounded with the electronics that he had repaired. He would rather just stay back here and have someone take care of the front desk. He would have someone to talk to during the quiet times in the shop. Yeah, that would be nice, he thought, to have a girl working out front that he could talk to. It was all nonsense, a stupid thought and he knew it. He started to get a rent payment ready for Walter. He would have to do a lot more business to afford a helper, more business would raise more suspicion and would land him right into the question he was trying so hard to conceal, "Who are you?" He didn't want that, no, he went through a lot of trouble to set himself up without having to explain who he is or where he came from.

Click, clack, click, clack, Diane walked through the front glass doors and proceeded right past the front desk then past the security desk.

"Your pass," one of the guards said. She turned and smiled at him as she walked past and he said, "Oh, never mind," then turned to his partner and lied, "I know her, ah, I remember her."

A Touch of Love

She walked down the hall of glass front offices and stopped at her boss's office. She knocked on the glass door, even as she saw she was being waved in. "Ms. Winchester" was not only on the door, it was on her desk and on the pass hanging from a chain around her neck. "I've been waiting for you," she said with a half-smile. Diane quickly glanced at the clock and saw 8:02.

"Sorry," she said as she sat down. "No, no, it wasn't long, I just need this meeting for my report," she explained. "How exactly is it going out there?" That is exactly how she would ask, how 'exactly' is it going? She went exactly by the book.

"It's going just fine!" Diane answered. "We've been set up for almost a week and the recordings are all clear. I haven't cut any tape for you as I'm still learning the players and our subject hasn't showed up yet. After we tape him, I'll make you a demo and give you something more complete."

"Well okay, I guess I'll just have to wait," Ms. Winchester said harshly. "How's Kurt?"

"Kurt? He's fine, I guess, he's in the van now, probably waiting for me to show," she quipped. "I don't think I mentioned coming in to the office to him." Diane hated this meeting already. As Mrs. Winchester droned on and on expounding on Kurt's talents and achievements in the Investigative division, she pondered that it might be Kurt himself that was ahead of her for a promotion.

"Yes, Kurt really knows his way around the equipment," she piped. "He helps to film hours and hours of video and recordings for me to produce into a report that will give you the information you need to continue the investigation."

As much as she wanted to say 'but', she held her tongue and asked if there were any other important finds and information developing on any other projects.

"Not that I can share," was the stern answer.

The phone started flashing and broke the pause created by the answer. "One second," she said as she pointed at Diane, "Investigation Division superintendent Ms. Winchester. Can I help you?" she answered. "Yes, it's Miss Wesson," she paused. "Yes, she's in my office now. Okay, I'll tell her." As she hung up the phone, she started telling Diane that it was Henry Stevens, her boss, that wanted to see her when they were finished. "You are to report to the upstairs conference room at nine thirty, for employee sensitivity training, so don't let him whittle away your whole day." She scoffed. "If you have time, stop back here before you leave." "Well, go!" she motioned. "Go see what Henry wants. Don't forget the meeting upstairs." Diane was already moving towards the door.

Joe flipped the sign and was surprised to see at least three customers waiting just outside. They bustled in and Joe asked them, "Who's first?"

A young girl stepped up and showed him her tablet. "It won't go sideways anymore," she explained.

"What do you mean sideways?"

"It used to turn sideways when I turned it and it doesn't anymore."

"Oh! That's just a setting, let me show you." Joe found and changed the setting, then told her there was no charge and she was so happy she skipped out the door. Just as he said next, Walter came in for his rent payment. Joe immediately went to the back room and retrieved the envelope.

He came back out and they stepped to the side and Walter whispered, "It's all here?"

"Yes, I got it ready earlier," said Joe. Walter left and Joe returned to his customers

The two other girls smiled and giggling asked Joe if he could fix their phone, hoping he would fix it free too. "I'll try," he told them. They told him they dropped it into the pool and even after drying for three days it still wouldn't turn on. Joe smiled at the still giggling teens and said, "Be right back," as he stepped into the office. Blink, the phone turned right on. He waited a few minutes and took the phone back to the girls. "Here you go, good as new," he explained. "Just keep it out of the pool, okay?"

"You're the best," one exclaimed as both rushed around the counter and gave him big hugs. "Is ours free too?"

"Yeah, yeah, okay," he said. "Just get back from behind the counter so people don't start to think it's a thing."

"Thank you," they said in unison, and preceded to skip to the door. Once outside one of the girls' moods changed and she shouted back at the store.

"You shouldn't be allowed to pick and choose who pays and who doesn't."

"No!" yelled the other. "It's not fair!" and they proceeded on their way.

In the van, Kurt had caught it all. Both the man and the payment, well, the envelope with the payment inside was recorded plain as day, but he was focused on the three girls. They don't like you, he thought, they probably like someone more like me, he fantasized.

A Touch of Love

Diane freshened up and proceeded to the department chair's office. Henry Stevens greeted her at the door, hand outstretched. A slight smile on his face, he greeted her, "Come in, come in, have a seat, how was your meeting with Ms. Winchester, rattled you a bit I suppose, I saw you in there and figured I'd give you an escape route. But really, how are you doing in the field with Kurt? We need good people in the field! But we need good people here coordinating their efforts too! I just want you to know your work has not gone unnoticed." He paused for a breath.

Diane quickly blurted, "We're doing fine out there. Kurt is okay in his own way, and he gets the tape, he does get good tape. We'll crack this case soon, I'm sure!"

"As I expect," Henry said, "wrap this one up, put a bow on it and then come see me. The battle-axe is due to retire soon and we'll need someone ready and field tested, if you know what I mean."

"I believe I understand," she replied.

Henry started talking about himself and how he got to his position and droned on and on

At one point Diane stood up and admired the large leafed plant, caressing it gently as she replied, "Oh, now that's interesting." She bent down to feel a smaller plant and thought, I just might get this promotion soon. He's handsome enough and dresses well, but he's just too old and stuffy. Yuck, I can't take too much more of him. Saved by the bell, the phone interrupted him, it was Ms. Winchester reminding him Diane needed to be at the sensitivity meeting at 9:30.

Henry stood up and got the door as she left, ending the meeting with, "Remember, call me! Now go, I don't envy you going to your next meeting. So boring!"

Jimbo saw the dust before he saw his brother's car as it came down the long drive to the plant. He was a bit excited about any news from Joe. He was disappointed when Walter just said, "Nope, didn't talk to him at all. He had customers, go get the dough yourself next month, talk all you want!"

"No, no," Jimbo said, "keep it like it is." Jimbo reached into the paper bag and counted out some money and gave it to his brother. "Really Walter, thanks for doing this for me."

"Your business," Walter said as he left. Jimbo stood there with the bag in his hand, best to let him wonder about Walter rather than me, he thought, Joe is my best friend.

Back in the van, Kurt was making tape but his attention was more on the scope he had pointed at the hotel across the street. That and Diane's station pointed directly at the parking garage. He alternated between the two as he grumbled about her being late again. Is she even coming at all today? he wondered.

"I want to punch something," she muttered after coming out of the boring sensitivity meeting. But she felt great and in her environment. She looked around and really didn't want to leave, but she headed for her car.

Walking past the guards, one motioned for her to come over. "Are you hungry?" he asked. "I'll be happy to show you to the cafeteria. I'm going there myself now for lunch. C'mon, it's on me."

She stopped and looked at a handsome man in a uniform, "Sure," she replied. "Thank you, thank you very much." He walked her down the nearby hallway and entered a large bright eating area. "Nice," she said. "You know you don't have to pay; I was going to stop soon for lunch anyway," she told him as they looked over the foods that were available.

"It would be my pleasure," he said.

They made their picks and the food looked great. This was not a second-rate establishment, well, for a cafeteria.

They sat down and he immediately started to eat hungrily. She watched quietly as she nibbled some salad. I love that uniform, she thought, he's quite handsome and is very polite. If he comes up for air, maybe we can get to know each other a little.

He didn't. It seems he didn't even look up or notice her until his plates were completely empty. That's okay, she thought, he was probably very hungry.

"How long have you worked here?" she asked.

"Fifteen years," he said. He then proceeded to tell her his whole sad childhood. He continued with some horrid teen years only to end up here with a chip on his shoulder because he hasn't made it to be a real cop yet. She almost left right there when she got the opening, but needed to give him a second chance to be even somewhat charming to her.

"Do you always carry that gun?" she peeped. She ate quietly as he spent another fifteen minutes explaining that it never leaves his side or his sight. Enough is enough, she thought and said thank you and goodbye as she hurriedly set off for the parking lot.

As she was leaving, he loudly announced, "Next time you come in I'll call my wife and maybe you could come over for dinner?" Diane never looked back.

The road back to work at the van was long, lonely, uneventful, boring and sad. I should be happy, she thought. It looks like I'll finally get the promotion I deserve. But she wasn't happy at all. She was going back to Hope, without any hope. Hope to find some real happiness in her life.

Chapter 4

Smith and Wesson

Joe leaned on his elbows with his head in his hands. The afternoon was quiet, too quiet. The afternoon was long, lonely, uneventful, boring and sad. As he watched a pretty girl walk down the sidewalk towards the store, he wondered if he would ever find his past and try to live a normal life. It was at this moment, Joe had either another lucky break, or a very unlucky break. Diane walked into the store.

Diane finally made it back to Hope. She parked and got out and literally charged towards the van. If he messed with her equipment, she would just be able to get it set up, then have to tear it down for the weekend. As she walked, she raised her hand and gave Kurt the finger, but was really hoping he hadn't turned her scope to watch her. Who am I kidding? she thought. He sees me right now, and then she gave him the finger again.

Kurt smiled broadly and waited to open the door for her. He was surprised that she was angry with him for monkeying with her stuff.

"Have you been working at all today?" she scolded.

"Hey, hey, hey, where you been? I've been here all day!" he replied. "The question should be had you done any work today?" Diane angrily explained that she had been at headquarters all morning. "Did you have fun?" he asked.

"Yeah, real fun, you should take the sensitivity class like I just did!" she quipped. "Hand me that laptop! Since you screwed up my stuff, I'll have to go out on my own here and get something done." Diane took the laptop and threw it down. She opened it and it started up, so she threw it again harder. This time it didn't make a peep. "Good, open the door and be sure to keep the cameras running. You can do that right?" she demanded.

"Sure thing, Doll," he replied while thinking, boy she sure is a bitch today.

Diane left the van and marched down the street towards the computer repair store. As she walked, she began to regain her composure and began to ease her stride. It's a beautiful day, she thought, I really hadn't noticed how nice it is out here. Smiling, she wondered if he was watching her walk towards his store and her gate smoothed even more. Oh yeah, she thought, just an ordinary person walking down the street, clack, clack, clack, an ordinary person in a great looking dress. Her smile widened.

Diane opened the door and walked in. As she approached the counter, she noticed his smile. He has a very nice smile, she thought, he's very good looking too.

"Problem with your laptop?" he asked as she held it out for him.

"It won't start up," she answered.

"I can look at it tonight," he replied. "I have a few others to fix in front of it. Unless you need it right away! I can prioritize it for you if you want!"

"No," she said, "it's important and all, but I can wait and pick it up Monday?"

"Great," he stammered, "I look forward to seeing you Monday. Just one minute and I'll get you a ticket." He took the broken laptop into the back office. He wrote 'Pretty Girl' on a piece of tape and affixed it to her laptop, realizing that he hadn't even remembered to ask her what her name was. I'll remember pretty girl, he thought to himself. Joe quickly returned and handed her the ticket. "I forgot to ask your name," he said. "For the ticket, you know," he stumbled.

"That's okay, it's Diane, Diane Wesson, w, e, s, s, o, n. I'll be back Monday, see you then!" she said, as she wheeled and headed towards the door.

"Let me get that,' said Joe as he hurried to beat her to the door. He opened it, held it and said, "Have a nice afternoon!"

"Thank you!" she smiled back, "Thank you very much."

As she walked towards the van, she decided she was going to have a nice afternoon. Walking right past the van, she headed for the parking garage. I'm going to go buy a new dress, she thought, that's enough work for today, I need to buy a dress, yes, a new dress for Monday. She continued walking, knowing that both of them were watching her.

Diane's weekend passed in a blur. Cleaning and rearranging, she tackled the whole apartment with newfound energy. She had just finished hanging the new drapes she had bought when she purchased her new dress, and she sat down for a rest. She picked up the novel she had been reading then tossed it down thinking, no, not today! I'm not reading about someone else's romance today! It's my turn! She went into the kitchen and made a cup of tea, then carried it to the bay window seat. She sat there peering out into the sunshine, carefully watching the people visiting the park.

Yes, she thought, it's my turn.

Saturday afternoon, Joe closed the shop and headed for the bus station. Jimbo hadn't ever come to visit him at the shop but he had gone to the recycling depot almost every other week to visit Jimbo. The bus ride wasn't long and Joe enjoyed it, staring out the window. Everything flew past in a blur except one sign, "Hypnosis, remember your past," and it was gone. It had hit him slowly, and by the time Joe realized it might be important, he was almost to the scrap yard. Where did I see that sign, he thought? Did it say what I thought it said?

It was a long walk to the yard, but it was a beautiful sunny day. Jimbo waved from a distance. Jimbo had been hoping Joe visited today. He had a lot to show him and he had some stuff only Joe could fix for him.

He rushed up and shook Joe's hand. "Good to see you," he barked, "got a lot of stuff to show you!"

Jimbo's fingers felt big in his hand. He was wearing three pairs of gloves today, probably picking out things for me; he didn't like to do that but he wanted to be ready with some stuff in case Joe came by.

"How's the computer repair shop coming along?" Jimbo asked.

"Great!" Joe replied, "Quite great. I had a real pretty girl for a customer yesterday, can't get her out of my mind!"

"Well, that is good news Joe! You really need to get out more, meet new people, have a life for gosh sake."

"And what about you?" said Joe.

"Oh, I have my days, and of course nights." Jimbo chuckled, "Not to worry about me, Joe, I'm getting by just fine!"

"I mean settling down, getting married, having kids!" said Joe.

Jimbo grinned, "Wait a minute there, Joe, I love my work, don't need no mother hen telling me what to do all the time. Ha, ha, ha, ha." They both laughed together. They went on smiling, talking, and laughing for hours as Joe fumbled and caressed the many electronic items Jimbo had gathered.

As it got late, they parted and Joe headed off for his room. He always stayed overnight as Jimbo had left everything like it was when he worked here. Joe had fixed it up real nice and when he finally went to bed, it felt a lot like being home.

The next morning, Joe had his coffee and wandered around the scrap yard. He always stayed on the junk side but today he wandered around on the metal scrap side. Piles of twisted scrap metal sorted into unusual-shaped piles, some quite large, as a huge crane loomed overhead. There were lots of machines to cut up metal and even a machine that crushed cars into little blocks of steel.

"Hey Joe! Come on over here!" yelled Jimbo. Jimbo didn't work on Sunday, the place was closed, but he liked coming around anytime Joe was here for a visit. "You really ought to stay out of that section, it's mostly dangerous. I don't even go over there unless I absolutely need to check on something important. I got special guys that work over there. They're a breed of their own, they work as a team. A regular guy could get hurt, get hurt bad, even killed if something goes wrong. Come on, I brought donuts and coffee, good coffee not the stuff you make! Ha, ha, ha." They were laughing again already.

Later that day, Joe picked through some of the piles looking for salvage when he spied a little wooden box. He picked it up and lifted the lid. Nothing happened. Broken, he thought, tossed out and forgotten. What a shame. He looked at the bottom and saw a small screw. Holding it with his thumb, he lifted the lid again and a beautiful ballerina popped out. The music played as it spun around and around. Yes, this is still good, he thought.

He took it to the bench and polished the case, just a few strokes of touch up paint and some detail polishing on the ballerina and it looked like new. I'll take this to the shop, he thought. He went to Jimbo's office and they said their goodbyes as Joe left. During the bus ride back, Joe made sure to watch for that sign, but to no avail. It was nowhere to be found.

Diane readied herself for bed. As she left the bathroom, she looked at her new dress hanging in her bedroom doorway. She could see her dress hanging there from almost anywhere in the apartment and she had glanced at it often. Every time she saw it, she thought of Joe. He really was nice, she thought to herself. She caressed the fabric as she walked by and got into bed. She was looking at her new dress when she drifted off to sleep.

Joe went into his store and quickly slipped into the office without turning on the lights. He sat the jewelry box down next to his bed. He went to his bench and started a few of the computers that were due to be picked up Monday, especially Diane's. It started just fine, all of them did. Some started up faster than expected. He got into bed and picked up the music box. He played it over and over, lulling himself to sleep. I hope the opportunity comes up to give it to her, he thought, I think she will really like it.

Chapter 5

Cutting the Tape

Kurt parked the van further away than usual. The zoom lenses were working well and there hadn't been any obstruction problems, so further away meant less of a chance to get noticed. He adjusted Diane's scope towards the parking garage. He then wandered his scope around, looking for anything of interest. Kurt was looking for anything interesting, not a promotion like Diane. Kurt loved his job. He couldn't care less about any of the politics of his work. He just liked the equipment and the job of surveillance. Guilt or innocence was not his concern, getting good clear tape and not getting exposed were his only concerns. Well, except looking around. Kurt was a bit of a pervert when it came right down to it. He thought it was well hidden but Diane knew. She had found her scope pointed at a window once and wondered what he was watching there. She also had peeked through his a few times when she got the opportunity and saw that it certainly wasn't a work target. She let that stuff slide though because he always got the tape she needed, he really got great tape.

Joe got up early, refreshed and happy. He showered, dressed, putting on his favorite shirt. He took his freshly made coffee to the counter and opened the store. He was looking for her already. A few customers trickled in and out. There were more than usual, but Joe really didn't notice that. He was thinking about Diane and alternating between looking out the window and gazing at the music box that he hoped to give her.

Diane slept in. She didn't set an alarm as she didn't want to seem to be anxious or overbearing. I'll pick it up before noon, she planned. She primped and dressed all morning. She posed over and over in the full-length mirror. It'll be like taking candy from a baby, she mused. She smiled broadly, who am I kidding, it's hard to take candy from a baby! They hold on tight and if you get it from them, they squawk to high heaven. "I will hit him with both barrels!" she mumbled, and she thought up a new analogy, "Beauty and charm is my plan." It was around ten-thirty when she finally took off for Hope.

Diane saw the white van, Kurt saw Diane coming, Joe saw Diane coming and Diane saw Joe was watching as she walked confidently towards the computer shop. Joe held open the door for her as she entered the shop.

"I saw you coming," he murmured.

A Touch of Love

"I see!" she replied.

"Your laptop is fixed," he told her, "Works just fine now."

"Great!" she replied. "How much do I owe you?" as she reached for her credit card.

Joe quickly said, "Nothing, nothing at all," as he tried to avoid turning down her credit card. "It was an easy fix," he explained. "Just a loose wire. Here, go ahead and try it," he offered.

Diane turned it on and it purred to life. "Oh great, this is my work computer and I dropped it. Now, I won't have to explain anything to my boss."

"There's more good news," Joe explained, "Your free repair comes with a warranty and a free cup of coffee if you join me for lunch at the café next door!"

"Well, goodness, lunch?" she stammered.

"If you wish," Joe replied.

"Tell you what," Diane said as she regained her composure, "Only if you let me pay. I have to repay you for fixing my laptop somehow, my company will pay for lunch."

"You drive a hard bargain," Joe said happily.

And so, they were off to lunch. They had parlayed their second meeting into a date.

Lunch went smooth, very smooth. Both desperately tried to keep it that way. Diane kept reminding herself to use charm, and Joe mostly listened attentively. She told him about her apartment and the view of the park, and mentioned her field work and desires for a promotion. He talked about working at the recycling plant with Jimbo.

A Touch of Love

Yes, lunch had gone well, when Joe spoke up and said, "We ought to do this again!"

"Yes," Diane answered, "Next week?"

"Sure," Joe replied, "Wait, we could make it Friday?"

"Friday?" she said. "Well, okay, I guess, Friday it is!"

As they left, they both stood on the sidewalk in front of the shop and looked at each other, waiting for what was next.

Diane broke the pause by saying, "Well okay, I'll stop at your shop Friday."

"I'm looking forward to it. Good bye for now, I had a great lunch!" he spoke.

"Me too," she answered, and with that, she wheeled around and walked back towards the van.

A Touch of Love

As Diane approached the van, she hesitated and darted into a little candle shop instead. Best kill some time in case he's still watching me, she thought. She spent the next half hour smelling the scents and looking at the beautiful candles, buying a few as she shopped. I feel wonderful, she thought. Suddenly, that thought faded and she realized that she had to get to work, and quickly! She had to arrange and cut all the tape, and get this case finished before Friday! She had to show Joe innocent of wrongdoing, point the finger at the real culprit, and wrap this case up. I must get to work, she thought, and now!

Diane stepped out and proceeded to enter the van. "Where have you...?" but Diane cut Kurt off right there.

"Gather up all the tape!" she ordered. "Be ready to wind up our surveillance here. I'm going to start cutting tape and I'm pretty sure my submission will end this assignment."

Kurt turned off all the equipment, securing the cameras for travel and jumped into the driver's seat. He drove into the parking garage, flashing his badge for entrance. At her car he helped her transfer the tapes into her car and waited for her to say something, realizing this might be the last time they work together for a while. He smiled at her.

She calmly said, "Move the damn van so I can go!"

Once home, Diane kicked off her heels, as usual, and poured a glass of wine. She sat down and picked up her half-read novel and after reading a few pages, threw the book down exclaiming, "You're doing it all wrong! I'll show you how to have romance! It's my turn."

She got up and went to her desk. She carefully got tape after tape out of the box and put them in order. This is going to take a while, she thought. Then she noticed that Kurt had marked some of the tapes as important. One even said, Rent Payment. "Kurt! You did something right for once!" she said aloud. "This will make it much easier for me." Knowing that, she retired to bed.

Diane woke up early and made herself coffee. She went to her desk and got an early start. While sipping her coffee she played the tape marked 'Rent Payment'. It started off with the girls waiting outside the store for it to open. Joe came to the door and let them in and they were bouncing all around. Joe was with one of them and soon she gave him a big hug. She stared at her phone by the door. It appeared that Joe took a phone from another girl, but then a well-dressed man came in and Joe went into the office and came out with an envelope. He gave it to him and that was it. All the work for that? she thought. She continued watching, hoping there was more to it. Joe took the phone into the backroom, and one of the girls went behind the counter and put her ear to the door. She bolted back and Joe came out, motioning them from behind the counter. They proceeded to give him big hugs, irritating Diane. They went outside, and Diane noticed they were now angry and shouting at the store door. Good! she thought. Let's not get quite so friendly. I wonder what he said to them as they left?

Diane poured through the tape all day long, stopping only for short breaks to eat and drink. She had almost made it through half when her eyes couldn't take anymore and she gave up for the night. Sixteen hours straight, definitely a record, time to get some sleep. As she lay there winding down, she couldn't help thinking about the many people that seemed to leave the store mad. Mostly men but even some women seemed angry when they got outside the store. Diane really wanted to know what the reason was, as she had gone into the store and when she came out did not have the slightest bit of anger in her. What was going on? she thought, as she drifted off to sleep.

Joe's week went slow. Customers came and left but nothing of note happened. Joe did have the music box to look at and listen to. It reminded him of the upcoming Friday date and gave him reason to smile.

Kurt, on the other hand, was busy. He had gone to a ballgame, visited the bar, ordered pizza for a movie he watched and, in general, screwed off. Now, he had to get to work writing a report for Ms. Winchester. I got this easy, he thought, she likes me, girls usually like me. He wrote how everything went smoothly, how he got the tape, and how well he and Diane worked together. Everything went smoothly; he wrote; I hope we have a chance to work together again!

It was almost ten o'clock when Diane was awake enough to get back into the tapes. It was on the way to the desk, carrying a fresh cup of coffee, that she noticed a tape that had fallen onto the floor. It was marked "Important". She watched as a guy went in and dropped off a computer, then left. Nothing unusual there, she thought. Then she saw the yellow hardhat guy walking down the sidewalk. I remember him, she thought, he sure left happy! But she still watched intently. Yes, he was very happy when he left the store, but wait, he went back into the store? I don't remember that at all. When he came out the second time, he was indeed angry, just like Kurt implied. She watched that tape over and over, he's happy, he comes back in for something, they shake hands and he leaves unhappy? Over and over, she watched it, until it hits her. She hurriedly puts on a tape she had already watched and fast forwards it. The customer shakes hands and then leaves angry. Tape after tape, she discovers that it is the handshake that is causing the anger. It's not anything he says, it's when he touches them, that seems to be what causes all the anger!

Diane got up to think about what to do. Should she tell him? And if yes, how? Do I come clean from the beginning? she thought. First, I must clear him and end this investigation. Then maybe? Wait, she pondered, Joe has never touched me. She thought hard, he has never even brushed against me. He has been a perfect gentleman this whole time. She sat down with a glass of wine. Did I just ruin the first time we hold hands? she wondered, and the first kiss? Oh no, oh no, you aren't doing this to me. You are not ruining this for me! She looked at the unread novel. I'll fix this! This can be fixed! I sure hope it can be fixed.

On Thursday, Diane wrote the final report for the surveillance. The report focused on the fact that he didn't have very many customers. She turned the spotlight on the man who collected the rent as opposed to Joe. She highlighted the fact that the rent collector came and went only caring about the envelope, and didn't concern himself with what was going on, or the management. She concluded that the store was at break even if that, and that the business wasn't even a business at all, and was better classified as a hobby. There, she thought to herself, this should get them off investigating Joe. The IRS did not like to waste time and money on a situation that didn't have any money that they could demand or seize.

She sent a copy of her report with the attached files and videos to Ms. Winchester, and blind carbon copied it to Henry Stevens, for good measure.

Chapter 6

Starting Over

Diane pondered about what to wear all morning. He dresses normal for his job, and I don't want to become a spotlight, or overdress. She settled on a pink lacy top. Her white jeans would go well with it, and her white heels would top the outfit off. More comfortable and more casual, that was the key.

On arrival to Hope, she almost pulled into the parking garage, but wheeled around and headed towards the shop. "Why not!" she proclaimed. She pulled into the 'customer only' parking spot. She entered the store at precisely twelve o'clock.

A Touch of Love

"Well, hello!" Joe announced, "I was afraid that you would forget about our lunch date!"

"No, I didn't forget at all, I was looking forward to it. So much I took the day off."

"You did?" Joe asked. "If you don't have to go back to work, do you want to do something a bit different?"

"Like what?" she questioned.

"Well, you could help me finish up and I can fix some computers, then I could close early. That way we could go have a nice dinner together. I even have a package of cookies to munch on instead of lunch."

"I think I would love that," she answered, "what do I do?"

Joe instructed her to stand behind the counter and when a customer came in, take the phone or laptop, make a ticket with their name, address and phone number, and tear off the ticket and give it to them for a receipt.

"Be sure to remind them, cash only," as he pointed to the big sign above their heads.

"Sounds great, my first day on the job," she joked.

She stood there looking over the store and through the glass wall at the city. This is nice, she thought, helping people, instead of trying to get them in trouble. Giving them smiles instead of frowns. It lasted only a moment. The door opened and a mother with two young boys came into the store.

"This tablet has been broken for quite a while. I've been waiting to be able to get it fixed. It just quit turning on. And now my phone has quit as the boys were fighting over it and it landed in the toilet. Can you help me?"

A Touch of Love

"Well, I'll see," Diane answered. "Fill out this ticket with your name and number, okay? I'll take the phone into the back and see if Joe has time for it."

"Oh, thank you," the woman said.

She took the phone back to Joe and explained the sad story. Joe looked her straight in the eyes.

"Watch this!" he said. A blue spark from his hand covered the phone. It lasted just a second or so. Joe pushed the button and the phone powered right up. "Take this to her and ask her to make sure everything still works! Tell her no charge."

She took the phone, wheeled around and took it to the woman waiting. With wide eyes, she said, "He fixed it! Check it out, be sure it works right."

"It seems to be fine," she said, "Oh, I'm so relieved." She didn't need to say that, as Diane could see it in her eyes.

"No charge!" Diane told her, "But leave the tablet, it will be ready next Tuesday." Diane took the ticket, pasted it onto the tablet, and said, "See you Tuesday," as the woman left.

Diane stood at the counter. She replayed the blue spark jumping from his finger to the phone, over and over in her mind. Four more customers came in over the next couple hours, each one dropping off their broken computer or phone, explaining what was wrong and taking their ticket as they left. Not one person had gotten angry, she thought, He's lucky to have me around. And she grew a great big smile. For a boring job, the time flew by. Joe had come out to check on her a few times, each time they exchanged small talk. He had even remembered to bring out those cookies and Diane munched on one as she realized that she didn't tear off the receipt and give it to the woman with the two boys. Oh well, she'll remember where she dropped it off, or I will call her and remind her.

Joe finally came out of the office and looked at her smiling and said, "Dinner?"

"I'm famished," she told him.

He held the door open for her and flipped the sign to closed. They had small talk as they waited for their meals. Both worried about the discussions soon to come. Him about the blue spark and her about explaining how she already knows about it. Dinner came and it was perfect. They ate and talked. She told him that she worked for the IRS, but nothing more, she explained some parts of her job and described her apartment. He listened. Diane watched as he took a bite of food, carefully dabbed his lips with the napkin, then listened intently. He's wonderful, she thought.

Joe told her about the music box. He talked about how he fixed it specifically for her. He told her he played it anticipating the current date. He told her she should get it and take it home.

"It needs a fresh start of love," he soothingly remarked. "It's very beautiful and it deserves a new start."

"Oh, yes, don't we all," she smiled.

The walk home turned dangerous as on two occasions Joe got too close for comfort. Diane was not going to let him touch her, not yet at least. The night was perfect and she planned on keeping it that way. They went into the darkened store and Joe put on a small light at the waiting area. Diane sat down in one of the chairs and Joe on the other side of the table. The music box was in the middle.

"Go on," Joe told her, "Open the lid." As she opened the lid, the ballerina rose up and started to spin. The music from Love Story started to play and it brought tears to her eyes.

A Touch of Love

Joe arose without saying a word and went into the office, giving her time to compose herself. He returned with two glasses and a bottle of wine.

Pouring her wine he said, "There's something I have to explain."

"Me first!" Diane said, her voice cracking, "It's all a lie!" she blurted out. "I broke the laptop on purpose! I really do work for the IRS and I was investigating you! I'm so sorry," she sobbed.

He looked into her eyes and calmly said, "Well, did you do a good job?"

"No!" she pouted, "well yes, oh, I don't know!"

She explained to him how she made it look like this was only a hobby, and that the man that picked up the rent was a better target.

"Walter?" he asked.

"They don't know who he is," she explained.

"Oh well, I guess it's my turn?" Joe said.

Diane interrupted him again, "No, that's not all. By watching the tape, I realized it's your handshake, your handshake makes people angry with you. You are losing all your good customers when you shake their hands. You know that blue spark? It's what makes people dislike you. I know it! I saw it happen over and over!"

Joe sat there with his mouth wide open. "Why didn't I pick up on that? How could I have missed it? It all starts to make sense now. I can explain," he said. "It all started in the desert." And he started telling her the whole story of his new life.

"You don't remember anything?" she asked as she quizzed him. "Mother? Family? Nothing? How you got that blue spark thing? Nothing at all?"

A Touch of Love

"That's right, nothing at all," Joe finished.

They sat there sipping wine for the next few minutes in silence. Finally, Joe asked, "What's next?" Diane thought a moment and then began to speak.

"Well, we need to find out who the hell you are! Then, we need to make this store and business legitimate and stop losing good customers. But what the hell are we going to do if you touch me and I get angry at you for no reason! And we both must decide if we want to do all this together."

"Hey, I'm cool!" Joe said as he pulled back into his chair, giving her more space. "And yes, I would love your company and help on all that stuff! You are the exact thing I have been missing in my life. I don't need any of the other stuff if I'm with you. Diane! I've fallen head over heels in love with you, can't you tell?"

"Yeah," she smiled, "I can tell."

A Touch of Love

They touched their wine glasses together and held them there for a long time, until she left.

A Touch of Love

Chapter 7

Quest for Answers

By Saturday evening, after hearing the music box play about a hundred times, Diane had made her decision. She emailed Henry Stevens, asking him for a leave of absence, and emailed Ms. Winchester explaining that she would be taking her two weeks' vacation, starting now.

Diane spent the day calling friends and some of her IRS contacts. I know people that can help, the question is, will they? Karrie! She remembered: I should call Karrie Barrett, she can find anybody!

Diane called Karrie, and they talked for a while about some of their college parties.

"Well, you didn't call me to talk about the good old days, so what up?" Karrie asked. Diane explained her problem and hoped Karrie could help find out about Joe's past. "That's not a good idea," Karrie explained. "Bad things can come out when digging into someone's past, especially the way I do it. My tools and searches are focused on criminal history and the like. Are you sure you would want that information?" Diane explained that she really didn't have a choice and she ended with the hint that he might be the real thing for her. Karrie knew that Diane would never say that if she didn't absolutely believe it was true, so they set up a meeting for Wednesday afternoon. "This place is a ghost town on Wednesday afternoon," she reported. "Everyone takes off early, so it will be a great time to do some searches." They agreed and ended with Karrie remembering the time when the wine bottle cork popped and hit the ceiling light, making the room pitch dark. "That's the first time I ever kissed Mitch," she admitted.

"Oh my goodness, that's so you!" Diane laughed, and they said their goodbyes.

Diane called Joe to give him the news. He quickly reminded her why she was falling for him when he said that he had been thinking of her all morning.

"I need to get another music box, only it will be for me, I need one too," he charmed. They talked about what Karrie might be able to do and when Diane finished, Joe brought up the sign he saw about hypnotism.

"Do you want to go look for the sign tomorrow?" Diane asked. "Can you get someone to run the store or can you close up for a bit?"

"There's a college kid that keeps asking me if I need help. I have his name and phone number around here somewhere. I'll call him today and see if I can show him the ropes," Joe answered.

Diane closed with, "Great, I'll pick you up tomorrow between 10:00 and 11:00 AM. Now the only important thing left is what to wear."

The next morning, Diane felt great; she even put the top down before heading out to pick up Joe. Hypnotist, spiritualist, or fortune teller, we should do whatever it takes to get to the bottom of this mystery, she thought. Why not? Why not go to a hypnotist?

She pulled up to the store and Joe was at the door. He seemed to be giving some last-minute instructions, then he came out smiling ear to ear.

"You look fabulous in this red convertible. I cannot believe you are here for me."

"You charmer," she quipped, laughing, "but thanks. I'll take the compliment. Where to?"

"Head out the State highway," he explained. "The sign was well out of town." The ride towards the recycling plant was smooth. Joe kept intently looking for the sign, stopping only to look at her and smile. She smiled back. They were doing something together and that was enough for Diane. As they neared the recycle plant, Joe became concerned. He looked at Diane and said, "I know I saw that sign last weekend." She approached the plant and started to enter the driveway. He quickly stopped her, "Let's not go visit Jimbo today," he said. They turned around and headed back to town. Joe was starting to get upset at himself; he had brought Diane out here on a long journey for nothing it seemed. They were, however, both enjoying the ride and the beautiful weather when Joe shouted, "Wait, go back!" Diane stopped the car and put it in reverse. She backed up about a hundred feet until Joe said stop. "Look out in that field," Joe said, "way out there, I think that's the sign. It's on the wrong side of the road and way out there where nobody can see it." He looked intently to read the sign but couldn't quite make it out.

"This is my job," Diane smiled and said. She opened the trunk, took out a go bag and opened it. In it was a collection of investigative tools. She grabbed a pair of binoculars and read the sign. "Hypnosis," she said. "Remember the past, and there's a number 814. Oh no, oh no, that can't be, oh no, it can't be that at all."

"What's the problem," Joe stammered. "What's the number?"

Diane looked at him with amazement. "That's our number," she said.

"What do you mean?" Joe asked, "What exactly is your number?"

"That's the IRS Clearing House number. If you call it, you'll get an answering service and they will direct you based on what you're looking for to the right office. They will then pretend to be associated with the subject that you are inquiring about. They work on the assumption that somebody undercover may be discovered. They're just going to get your name and address and contact information and tell you they will get back to you, and if you become a problem, they will send someone out to fix the damage. We certainly do not want to call that number. And I would love to know why it's on a sign that you would drive by and try to help you find your past."

Joe laughed aloud, "So the plot thickens," he remarked. "Well, that's one dead end. Any other ideas?"

"Sure, plenty," Diane replied. "Tomorrow we go see a friend of mine. He's sure to be a great help."

"You trust him?" Joe asked.

"Well, I hope so," she answered. "He's my ex."

"Oh great, let's go see your ex," Joe complained.

"It's not like that," she said. "That was a long time ago, and he married my sister. He'll help; he'll do everything he can to help me. And that means help you."

"Okay," Joe answered, "How about we stop for some dinner, and start out fresh again tomorrow?"

"That's a great idea," Diane replied.

After a very enjoyable dinner, Joe was back at the shop. "How did things go while I was gone?" he asked his new employee.

"Things went just great," Ronald replied. "Just great, look at all these computers and laptops I took in while you were gone. You can fix all these?"

"Sure, sure," Joe said. "I can fix all those. Were there problems or something you couldn't handle?"

"Nope, no problems at all. I handled it all. I even swept the floor," Ron retorted.

"Well, it seems you did an excellent job, Ron. What about tomorrow, are you free tomorrow? Or wait a minute, what about the rest of the week, can you do the same thing the rest of the week?"

"Sure," Ron said. "I'm free all next week too, if you need me?"

"Well let's settle on this week and we'll talk about next week later. If we have as much business as you did today in the coming days, I think the answer might be yes," Joe explained. Ron smiled at him and as he left, Joe made sure that he didn't shake hands with him. Let's keep him happy, he thought.

.

Chapter 8

A Day to Remember

Morning came quickly for Joe, and he crawled off the lumpy cot. He quickly showered, got some of the finished computers ready, and turned the store sign to open. Minutes later, Ron came, right on time. Joe was giving him instructions when Diane walked in.

"Are we ready?" she asked.

Joe replied, "Almost," and showed Ron the tablet that the lady with two children was to pick up. Diane reminded him that he may need to call her, and she didn't have a ticket.

Then she said, "Wait, never mind, I'll call her now!" She proceeded to call the customer. Joe was impressed and glad she was pitching in. Once finished, Diane and Joe headed off to the big city. They had a big day planned. Diane wanted to do some shopping and visit the sunken garden park before the first meeting with Karrie.

They were halfway there, in the middle of nowhere, when the car started acting up. Thump, thunk, thunk, it was much louder this time. Thunk, thunk, it went again, causing Diane to pull over. She saw a driveway with a parking lot, and pulled in. There was a small building, some cars and two school buses. Joe had just started to get out when the car started rocking fiercely back and forth. The rocking increased, and Diane, straining on the seat belts, almost fell into Joe's lap. She grabbed the steering wheel to steady herself and watched as a school bus rocked back and forth, then tipped completely over onto its side.

"It's an earthquake," Joe yelled. "Hold on tight. It'll be over soon," he calmed her as the car slammed back and forth. It seemed to last forever, but then it stopped as suddenly as it had started.

Some women were screaming in the distance. "Help!" Joe heard, as he saw them waving their arms.

"Come on, Diane, let's see what's wrong." They bolted over towards the women. Almost incoherently, one of them started to yell at them.

"You have to save the children; the kids are in the hole."

"What hole?" said Joe.

"This is an old missile site," she said. "Kids are on a field trip; they are in the bottom where the missile used to be. Come here and look, the elevators are completely broken. They're trapped, you must do something." Joe stepped into the doorway and looked down. It looked more like the opening for a root cellar, but as he stepped down, he saw that the area opened and was larger than it looked. There was a walkway and a railing, but the elevator had shaken loose and was broken. It had tipped sideways, obviously beyond repair.

"I don't know what you want me to do?" he shouted.

"It's broken all right, and there are kids down there?"

"Yes!" she screamed. "The kids are down there. There are more than 30 kids down there trapped. No one is answering the 911 call." Joe peered into the darkness down over the rail but couldn't see any children.

"Is there another way down there?" he asked.

"There is a great big door in that shack, it's supposed to go down, but it's locked," was his answer. "The elevator is the only way down, to go on a tour."

Joe was unable to do anything at this location, so he immediately scrambled out of the stairway and over into the old shack. It was dark and musty, but it had been the main entrance into the missile silo. The card reader that allowed entry into the building was undeniably broken. Joe approached, reached out and touched the card reader. Diane saw the blue spark and looked up as a small emergency light turned on. The light over the dark doorway started to blink red, blink, blink, blink; it turned yellow. Within seconds, the light turned green and a motor sound started, and Joe yelled for Diane to open the door. She lifted the large lever and pulled. Slowly, the old door creaked open. Everyone quickly went through and down the semi-circular cement stairs that seemed to encircle the silo. A short way down, the next level had a similar door.

"Open the door," everybody said, "open the door."

"Please step back," Diane pleaded. "Can you open the door, Joe?" she whispered.

"I'll try again," he said as he touched the broken card reader. Again, the emergency light came on and lights above the door flashed. Suddenly, they went to green and you could hear the motor open the latch that allowed the door to open. Again, Diane opened the door, and everyone went through hurriedly down the next set of stairs. That same type of door prevented them from entering the next level. Joe touched the reader, but nothing happened. The blue spark emanating from his finger had started to fade.

"Hurry, please!" the lady in the back said.

"He's doing the best he can," Diane reminded her, but again whispered to Joe, "Is everything going to be okay?" Joe paused, turned to look at her and took his finger off the card reader. "Everyone, please get back," he pleaded.

"Yes, give him some room please," Diane added.

Joe turned and touched the card reader again. On the other side of the door, the blue spark was inches shy of bridging the gap to the motor. Joe reached with his other hand and touched the reader with both hands this time. The emergency light flickered then came on. Everyone waited, holding their breath for the lights above the door to start to come on. Finally, a red light flickered, and then a yellow. But the green did not come on. Everyone waited but no green light. Incredibly, the motor sound started up and the door then let out a thump. Diane raised the lever and pulled. The door came open even though the green light had never come on.

"Damn thing must be burned out," Joe said. Everyone let out a sigh of relief and proceeded down the stairs.

"This must be the last one," Diane said. Joe looked at the door and the card reader and it appeared in good condition. Luckily, he touched the reader and a faint blue spark was enough to light the lights and open the door.

The door opened to all the children screaming, "Yay, we're saved," and "Thank you!" The women rushed past Joe and Diane and started hugging the children, explaining they're all okay now.

Once back up on solid ground, the kids piled in the bus that was still upright. The ones that didn't fit climbed into the cars and within minutes they were off to go back to the school, waving and thanking Joe and Diane as they left. "What do you bet the car fixed itself, Diane?" Joe smirked.

"I'm not betting against you on anything," she laughed.

This little escapade changed the entire morning. Now instead of doing some fun shopping and having a romantic walk in the park surrounded by beautiful flowers, they had to hurry to make their appointment with Karrie. They jumped in the car and took off.

Both were quiet until Diane piped out, "How do you suppose they're going to tell everybody how they got into the building? How do they think they got in the building? Who are they going to say got them into the building? And who are they going to say saved the children?" Joe didn't answer.

They arrived at Karrie's office a little late and she was glad. "It takes a while to get the place cleared out," she explained. With no one around, Karrie could ask Joe the questions she needed. "What day was it when you came out of the desert and how long were you in the desert if you can remember?" Joe started to explain his story but she stopped him, "I only need to know what I need to know." She input the date, subtracting a day, and searched for missing persons. She looked him over and put in 29 for his age. Joe started to argue, but she stopped him by saying it wasn't important what his real age was; the age that was important is what other people thought his age was. "I think that's 29," she said. Karrie asked him many more questions hoping to narrow down the search when it came back. "A nationwide search will bring up a lot of people, plus we can't rule out Canada or Mexico even. Although a Mexican search would probably be worthless, as their records are horrible," she explained. "Go have some lunch in the cafe while we wait if you want; the food's not bad and it'll be practically empty as everyone skipped out."

They had lunch and then returned to Karrie's office. "Boy, it doesn't look good," she said. "Of the two guys I found, neither fit your description, one is a bodybuilder, and the other weighed 300 pounds. Nobody else even comes close. I'll keep working on it, but I don't think you're going to get better information than this. Either nobody knows you're missing, or nobody wants to tell anybody." They both thanked her and invited her to come to dinner but she politely refused. "Got a thing I'm working on at home," she said. "I got to get it finished up before the weekend. So have fun and I'll let you know if I find anything new."

They had some free time so Diane pressed for them to go to the sunken gardens for a walk before dinner. Joe agreed and they walked the four blocks to the park. The flowers were beautiful this time of year, and you could smell them from a block and a half away.

"Boy, this is going to be a day to remember," Diane said.

"Yes, with the rescue and the earthquake and not being able to find out who I am, I think I'll be able to remember this," he laughed.

Diane looked right at him, smiled, and said, "Actually, you should have some pretty good new memories; maybe the old ones aren't worth looking for."

"I'm beginning to think you're right," he answered.

That night at dinner, Diane and her sister Susan talked and talked, catching up on all the old business. Dinner was finished by the time she got around to the first question to Thomas, her sister's husband.

"What do you know about a sign on Old State Road? It says 'hypnosis' then 'remember the past.' It's got our clearing house phone number on it!"

Thomas answered, "I don't know about it, but you should ask Freddy, you know, Freddy from the Christmas party."

"You mean the guy that almost got us thrown out?" Diane asked.

"Yeah, that's the guy. You should call him. I have his number; he knows everything about the clearing house. If anybody knows what's going on there, he will. Go ahead, call him up and charm him as only you can do." Susan quickly kicked him under the table. "Sorry about that," he said, "You know what I mean."

"What about the fixer, he wouldn't happen to owe you any favors would he?" Diane asked.

"He doesn't owe me any favors," Thomas answered, "but he doesn't have to. He's dating my sister! But that is all hush, hush. What kind of paper do you need?"

"Joe needs a whole makeover," she answered.

"Suppose you can make that happen?"

"Is the law involved?" he asked.

"No, no, nothing like that," Diane quipped. "Amnesia is all. Problem is, even Karrie can't find him. It doesn't look good. I think it's just best to go ahead and fix him, and if we ever do find out who he really is, well, we'll worry about that then."

The trip back to Hope was quiet. Both were thinking of the possibility of just quitting the quest for Joe's past. Joe had become clear on the probability that his past wasn't nearly as good as his present. He really was lucky and Diane seemed to be a dream come true. He realized that he very much wanted to go down this new path with Diane at his side. It was getting crystal clear that finding his past, no matter what it was, would likely screw up his new relationship. Diane was thinking very close to the same thoughts as Joe. I don't care about his past! He is a great guy! Even if his past wasn't perfect, he's great now, at least for me, he's perfect.

When they got to the missile silo, Diane slowed and pulled into the end of the drive. There was a temporary fence surrounding the entire facility. The bus that had been on its side was gone too.

"Well, that was quick," she said.

"Indeed," Joe replied. "I suppose the Army still has a stake in this, even though it's deactivated. Best to block it off, especially now."

They got back on the road and headed to Hope. Diane planned to drop off Joe and travel the half hour drive home. Since the big city hadn't had any damage or even reports about the earthquake, neither of them had even wondered if Hope suffered any damage because of the quake.

It took another hour and a half before they hit the outskirts of town, and it was now apparent that Hope had been shook pretty good. They could hear sirens and see the flashing lights on the side streets. Diane turned the radio on in hopes of news, but only music was playing on the normal channels. As she neared downtown, traffic got heavy and soon they were stopped. A traffic jam? In Hope, at this hour? Joe stood up in the car. The top was still down and from his height he could see a firetruck blocking the intersection.

"I'm going to see what's going on," he said as he got out of the car.

"Not without me!" she blurted, and they trotted up to the intersection. Sure enough, the huge fire truck was diagonally parked and blocking the whole intersection.

Joe yelled up to the driver, "Can I help?"

"It just quit, suddenly. I got nothing, no power, no lights, nothing!" he replied. "Are you a mechanic?"

"Not really, but maybe I can help!" Joe told him.

"Don't do anything dangerous," a fireman barked. He had approached Joe from the rear and Joe whirled to see him.

"Oh, I won't!" Joe told him. Joe reached into the grill area and fumbled around until he found a wire. With his other hand, he touched a screw on the headlight, the blue spark came to life and the lights on the truck flickered. He fumbled around more to grip another wire and the siren squawked to life and quit.

"You're getting it!" the driver yelled. Joe tightened his grip and the truck sprung to life. Lights were flashing and the siren was screaming. When the driver turned the key, the motor grumbled to life. The fireman standing next to Joe had seen it all and yelled over the noise that a building had collapsed and they had to hurry to the scene. "Thanks!" he yelled, as he jumped onto the truck and they quickly sped off.

They raced back to the car only to find a driver behind them blowing his horn. Not that he could hear her, but Diane was screaming back at him.

"What do you have to do? He just cleared the intersection for everyone! He probably saved lives helping to get the emergency fire truck to the scene of a collapsed building. He's saving lives and you can't wait for one second? You're an idiot!"

"Okay, okay, I'm not a saint Diane," Joe chuckled.

And she began to smile then laugh.

"Oh yes you are," she quipped, "and you're my saint!"

Diane headed to the store and as they passed the parking garage, they could see that the lights from the store were still on. As they pulled up it was apparent that a window had cracked and another had broken. Ronald was still there! He came out to greet them and explained about the earthquake damage.

"I figured I'd wait for you to return and protect the place," he explained.

"Thank you, thank you," Joe said. "Let's see the damage."

"It's mainly this big window!" Ronald showed him.

"Good thing the weather is so nice!"

"Yes, indeed, we are lucky the weather is cooperating. Do you need anything, Ronald?" Joe asked.

"No!" he answered. "I'm just glad you're back and that I did the right thing."

"Well, there isn't anything we can do tonight. The store alarm will go off if someone breaks in during the night. We can clean up and see about getting the windows fixed in the morning. See you then?" Joe asked.

"Sure, glad to help," Ronald answered.

"It's late now, so we'll get a late start tomorrow. Get your sleep; I'll see you when you get here."

"Okay, bye," and Ronald left.

"I have to get going too," Diane murmured. "It's late and I'm tired."

"You okay to drive?" Joe questioned.

"Oh, sure, but we have an even bigger day tomorrow because of this."

"Okay," Joe replied, "But drive carefully."

He leaned forward towards her but she wheeled around and quipped over her shoulder, "Not tonight, you have to keep both Ronald and me happy."

Diane started the car, and Joe stood in the doorway until the lights from the car faded into the night.

A Touch of Love

Chapter 9

Answers

Morning came quickly for both Joe and Diane. Joe started his day sweeping up glass, and Diane by calling Freddy about the clearinghouse number.

"Hello!" the voice on the phone answered.

"Hello," Diane answered, "Is this Freddy?"

"Yes, it is. Is this Diane?" Freddy replied.

"Yes!" she stumbled. "What, you recognize my voice?"

"Oh, yes, and caller ID. I got your number from Tom Springfield. I'm a bit miffed with you about giving me the slip!"

"I know Thomas but I have no idea about giving you the slip. What's that about?" Diane quizzed.

"You mean you didn't see me sitting in the back at that sensitivity class on that Monday? I looked all over for you afterwards, but you were nowhere to be found!" Freddy explained.

"No Freddy, I didn't see you nor did I pay any attention during that boring meeting. After the meeting I went to the cafeteria. I wasn't hard to find!" Diane continued to explain the boring security guard and boring lunch.

"The one place I didn't look!" Freddy exclaimed. "I thought you might still be mad about when you lit off that smoke bomb at Christmas!"

"It wasn't a smoke bomb and you know it!" she barked, "It was a stink bomb and it was you that lit and threw it!"

"Hmmm, maybe you're right, I guess it was me!" he laughed. They both cracked up about it.

"I guess it really was funny," she admitted.

"So why did you call me?" Freddy asked Diana.

"Well, Thomas told me to," she answered, "he said you knew all about the clearinghouse."

"Well maybe not all," he replied, "but what's your question?"

"What do you know about the sign on State Road that says hypnosis?" she asked. The phone went quiet.

Freddy finally broke the silence with, "What about it?"

"So, you do know about it!" Diane surmised.

"Yeah, I know about it," he said, "but what are you asking about?"

"Well, what the hell is it doing in the middle of a field a hundred yards off the road, for starters?" Diane probed.

"You saw that?" Freddy quizzed. "Okay, I did that."

"You did that?" Diane was getting puzzled so she said, "Can you explain the whole story to me?"

"I'll try," he answered. "I was the one that took that sign out there and set it up. They were looking for information on some guy that worked at the recycling center out there, in hope of getting information on the Rossi brothers. You heard of them?"

"Of course I have," she replied, "The agency has tried to pin them down on tax fraud for years."

"Well," he continued, "this guy that's not on anybody's radar, shows up out of the blue and rents this building owned by a conglomerate run by the Rossi's. So, we wanted to find out what he knew. All we knew was he had amnesia and we figured we could get the info from him without him even knowing. See, he would answer all our questions, thinking we were trying to help him remember the past. I thought the plan was brilliant, but then I got a memo telling me to immediately remove the sign. I know now, that it was because of your report, making him a dead end and instead they wanted to focus on Walter Thompson. Are you following me?"

"Yes," she answered, "very much so, go on."

"Well," he said, "Walter cracked like an egg dropped from a second story building. The guy is big and looks like he's a mobster, but he turns out clean as a whistle, and he's a really nice guy! He told us he only picks up the rent for his brother Jim Thompson, and that Jim just didn't want your guy to know it was him helping him out with the building lease. The investigation quickly turned to Jim 'Jimbo' Thompson, and Kurt is out there, as we speak, getting tape on Jim and the recycling operation. Okay?" he finished, "That's all I know. Don't repeat this, you're supposed to get this information from Winchester, not me, but I'm glad to help you."

"You helped me a lot," she exclaimed. "I had no idea this was going on."

"Maybe you should go see Kurt?" he asked. "Get out there, cut the tape. If we nail the Rossi's, well, everyone will get a raise! You cut the tape to convict the Rossi's and you're guaranteed to get a promotion. Maybe even boss over the battleaxe herself! That'll stir things up!"

"Thanks for everything Freddy, you don't know how much this conversation helped me, I really owe you for this. One last thing, why was the sign in the middle of a field?"

"That's on me," Freddy laughed. "I was told to get the sign down immediately, but I was in my Porsche. It wouldn't fit inside, so I carried it across the road, into a field and lay it on the grass. Someone, maybe the farmer, must have found it and stuck it in the ground. I ended up going back in a company truck to retrieve it."

"Ahh," she replied, "that explains everything. Thanks for enlightening me.

Another thing, I'm a bit embarrassed, I don't know your name. All I know is Freddy!"

"Chiappa," he stated, "Fredrick Allen Chiappa. It's hard to pronounce and hardly anyone knows it, so that's okay."

"Well thanks again," she ended. "I can't thank you enough." And with that the phone call ended.

Joe can't possibly be involved with the Rossi's, Diane pondered. Hell, he doesn't even know it wasn't Walter's building to rent, but it sure looks like Jimbo is involved. That will be very sad for Joe. Yeah, I have to go see Kurt.

The phone was still warm when it rang. "Hello?" Diane answered, there was no caller ID.

"Fixer," was the reply.

"Fixer? Is that your name?" she asked.

"Fixer will do," replied the mechanical voice. "Is this Diane Wesson?"

"Yes, it is! Thank you for calling, are you going to help me with Joe Smith, can we get him a past?"

"Wait," was the answer, "First, you must understand that everything will be confidential and nothing will ever be mentioned again. Next you must do nothing to discover who I am or how I work. Do you agree?"

"Yes," she answered, "I agree!"

"Okay then, you have a stellar record, people in high places are willing to vouch for you, I've done the research on you and you were easy. No controversy at all, just praise, so understand that your record is why I will give you this service."

"Thank you, thank you," she replied, "What do I have to do next?"

"Nothing at all," the voice replied, "Unless there is something you know I have to include in his past?"

"No, nothing as far as I know, he really doesn't remember anything and we don't even have any clues to follow. Even Karrie can't find anything," she answered.

"Wait for my call in a few days," the voice said, "I'll tell you where to meet." Click, the phone went dead. That was unusual, she thought, but we are finally getting some answers and making some headway.

Joe was just finishing the clean up when Ronald came in.

"Great timing, Ronald," he exclaimed! "I was just about to go into the back and make some calls."

"Go ahead," Ronald told him, "I'll finish with the clean up and take care of everything. I'm really in my element while

I'm working here, go, do your thing, I'll take care of everything else." He had barely gotten that out of his mouth when the first customer came in, then another and another. The afternoon was crazy busy. Many electronic items and computers were damaged in the quake. "When the electric goes off suddenly, many components can be damaged, you should have battery backup for this very reason," Ronald explained this over and over as the customers dropped off their items.

Joe finally got Walter on the phone. Joe explained the quake damage and asked Walter who to call.

"Oh, geez Joe, I don't know anything about your building. I hate to tell you this but it's been Jimbo running this deal all along. I just pick up the rent for him. He didn't want you to know it was him. I don't have anything to do with it or the deals he made to help you."

"Oh, wow, Walter, I never suspected," Joe said.

Walter continued. "He likes you Joe, and tell you the truth, so do I, I've watched Jimbo my whole life trying to fit in and, well, your friendship with him changed him for the good. He'd do anything to help you out and that's why I helped him. I hope you understand."

"Jimbo is my best friend," Joe replied, "and you've been a good friend too, don't worry, I'll talk to Jimbo and get it all straightened out."

"Thanks, pal," Walter said, and they said goodbye and hung up.

Joe sat there for a long time preparing to call Jimbo. He thought about how it all made sense now. How he had gotten a store with a backroom to live in, without any rules, without any paperwork or lease, low rent in a great location. All this he mistook for luck, when all along it was

Jimbo, shuffling the cards and dealing him a great hand. How else could a guy with no identification, no past, no bank, no credit, no anything, fall into this store and perfect deal? Jimbo was indeed a true friend.

During this pause, Joe started fixing some of the computers that Ronald had been bringing in the last few days. Things were starting to back up and he figured he better make some room for today's business. He fixed computers, some tablets and laptops, plus a few phones in the next few hours. Time went by fast as he had a lot to think about. He finished the last one that would fit on the 'Done' table, each one with a price and a note about what was repaired. He was just about to call Diane and ask her about what to say to Jimbo when he heard a commotion in the store. When Joe opened the door, there were four or five construction workers surrounding Ronald with papers to sign.

"We're here to fix the damage!" one of them blurted out. "We just need these signatures."

"Go ahead, Ronald, sign the papers for them!" Joe instructed.

Some of the guys immediately started to work as he signed. They worked quickly, and soon both the cracked window and the broken one were replaced with sturdy plywood. They did a good job, and for a patch, it didn't look half bad. Ronald had already stapled some posters and signage both inside and out. He really has ingenuity and is doing a great job for the store, Joe thought.

"The new windows will be installed next week," one of the workers explained. "We'll call you when we are on our way."

"Great!" Joe told him. "And thanks, thanks a lot."

Diane tried to call Joe. The phone had been busy and Joe didn't have call waiting. Joe had a landline phone because without a credit card he couldn't get a cell phone. This was fine with Joe, but now since she had to wait, she decided to go to the store and do the shopping she desperately needed. Other than the new dress, all her shopping had been put off. In her kitchen, she was out of most everything. She spent the day getting groceries and replacing all the little things in the house that needed replaced. It turned into a long exhausting day. She sat down and finally had time to call Joe again.

"Oh, hi Diane," he said cheerfully, hearing her voice.

"I got a lot done today," she told him. "We really got some answers too. I found out about the hypnotist sign, it's a long story I'll tell you tomorrow, I even spoke to the fixer, and things are going smoothly there. But right now, I have to tell you something I really didn't want to tell you."

"What's that?" Joe asked.

"I found out that you don't rent the store from Walter," she explained.

"Oh, I know that," Joe replied.

"Oh, wow, you know that?" she spoke.

"Yeah, I found out today," Joe told her. "Seems Jimbo has been running the deal all along, just didn't want to tell me. Walter just picks up the rent for him."

"Gee, I've been fretting telling you this news all day," she explained.

"How did you find out?" Joe asked her.

"Freddy told me!" she explained. "The guy that knew about the sign?"

"Oh, yeah, him," Joe replied. "What about the sign?"

"I'll explain that in detail when we're together," she answered. "Until then I've got to tell you that I'm going to try to get back to work."

"Oh, Jesus, is something wrong? Did I do something? Are you mad at me?" Joe kept prodding.

"No, no, no, nothing like that," she says. "I still love you, don't worry," and she giggled at him. "No, the investigation took a turn and the recycling plant is being surveilled. I guess Kurt's on the job now. I want to go back to work and find out what's going on. I want to be the one that cuts the tape so I can be sure that Jimbo hasn't been caught up in this unfairly. They're looking for some real bad actors and Jimbo just doesn't fit the bill from all I know about him. I got to get back in there so that we know what's going on."

"Oh, thanks," Joe told her. "Jimbo doesn't have a criminal bone in his body. I'd stake my life on it."

"I believe you!" Diane said. "But somehow, he's connected to this mess. I don't want to speculate so I figure I'll just try to get back on the team this Monday. Actually, I hope they let me."

"Okay," Joe finished. "The store is boarded up so everything's fine here. Again, don't worry about me."

"I'll worry about you if I want," Diane quipped back, again giggling as they said their goodbyes and goodnights.

Chapter 10

The Plot Thickens

Kurt sat in the dark quietly. He loved his job, but at this very moment he was lonely. Most of the time he was okay with being alone with the electronics, he was in his groove, but today he missed Diane, and he wished someone would show up soon to cut the tape. At times like these, lonely, he scanned the surroundings for something of interest, without any luck. Trees, trees and more trees, he thought as he swung the bucket around. He was indeed surrounded by trees. Trees, the sticks or out in the boonies, whatever you call it, Kurt was alone. The truck that he was in was a hollowed-out work truck from the power company. The inside of the back of the truck was filled with electronics, everything you could need. The bucket attached to the truck had a couple long-range cameras completely installed and invisible. The bucket was raised high against a power pole, completing the ruse. On the outside it appeared to be an old work service truck, but the inside was an electronic marvel. No one would think twice. He had also placed a camera in an old car, and positioned it outside the recycling plant driveway. Cars are parked there all the time, and no one would suspect anything. Another camera was in a tree and but for the high winds, it usually got good tape. The long-range zoom cameras could read the license plate on a car in the plant that was about to be crushed. Kurt loved these cameras and wished he had one for his own.

There were six hours to go until Kurt could wrap it up for the weekend. He spent his time working the cameras and changing tapes. He meticulously labeled each one with the time and date, but he always added anything he saw that was interesting or unusual. He didn't have to do that, but he knew it really helped the person cutting tape, and right now he really wanted a tape cutter to like him.

Diane started the weekend with a flurry. She cleaned and arranged her apartment in anticipation of Joe visiting. She scrambled around the apartment sorting and putting things away. When she got to the bedroom, she was ashamed of the mess. It wasn't dirty or anything like that, but it was littered with books and some food containers and empty bags were strewn about. This room is not for reading and eating, she silently proclaimed. No more, she thought. She tidied up, refusing to think about the fact that Joe wasn't going to stay overnight.

When everything looked just right, she got herself ready, jumped into the car and headed off to pick up Joe.

Joe spent the morning fixing and labeling the computers in the office. There were quite a few more than usual, and Joe was glad, as it would cover hiring Ronald and more. He got himself cleaned up and waited for Diane. The wait wasn't long at all; Diane picked him up, wheeled around the block and they headed towards her apartment. The ride was joyful. They sang to the radio together, they talked of wants and dreams, and were always ready to laugh.

When they arrived, Joe complimented her apartment. It was very nice and cozy compared to his office. He started thinking about how she was accustomed to living and what he may be able to provide for them. All kinds of ideas started going up in his head as he realized just how much more he could do if indeed the fixer could get him a new identity. It was time to discuss these new ideas with Ronald on Monday, he decided. In the meantime, Diane and Joe went to the farmers market. They strolled through the aisles as Diane bought fresh vegetables and fruits. Then they placed everything in the car, and went to dinner. Dinner was nice; as Diane sat there looking at Joe, she realized that Joe wasn't pretending on their first date. He really was interesting and attentive. She had enjoyed all the dinners with him, far more than any date she had had in the past. After dinner, they agreed she should take him back to the store. They both realized how close they were getting, how dangerous it was, and how it was best to wait. Upon dropping him off, they stood there, face to face, for a long time.

Joe broke the silence and said, "It's getting late, you better get back. Thank you, Diane, I had a wonderful day."

"Me too," she replied, "and I guarantee you it's only going to get better."

On Monday morning Diane immediately headed for IRS headquarters. When she arrived, she walked right past the guard, only giving him a smile. She headed straight for Ms. Winchester's office, knocking briskly as Ms. Winchester waved her in.

"Well hello, Diane," Ms. Winchester said, "Aren't you supposed to be on vacation?"

"That's what I came to see you about," Diane replied. "I want to cancel the second week of vacation and get back to work."

"Well, I'm quite sure you can't do that," Ms. Winchester answered. "There's no form to cancel a planned vacation, and as far as I remember, it's never been done."

"Isn't there somebody you could ask?" Diane asked.

"No," Ms. Winchester answered. "I'm in charge of all the people under me, and I take care of the vacations. The rules say that if you get granted vacation, you must take it." Diane looked at her and politely asked if she could ask Henry about it.

Ms. Winchester replied, "Sure, but I don't know what you think he might be able to do about this."

"Well, it won't hurt to ask," Diane replied, "I wanted to talk to him about something else anyway."

"Why, what's going on?" Ms. Winchester asked.
"Something I should be aware of?"

"No, no, no, nothing like that!" Diane smiled and chuckled, "No, it's not work related at all."

"Well, go see Henry then," Ms. Winchester exclaimed. "If he can help, I'll go along with it."

"Thank you," Diane ended, "I knew you'd try to help."

Diane swung open the door and headed straight for Henry's office. Henry was very happy to see her.

"Are you on vacation?" he asked.

"Yes!" she replied, "but I definitely want to get back out there. Is there any way you can cancel my vacation and get me back to the field?"

"Well, Diane," Henry said, "just what is going on that you of all people want back in the field and why is it such an imperative?"

"I heard that Kurt was out there by himself, not that I miss working with Kurt or in the field, but it sounds like he's onto something big and I don't want to let him down right in the middle of an investigation. Kurt is great at making tape but neither of us expects him to be able to cut it. I've heard that he's on to something big too. I'm talking raises and promotions big."

"I don't know where you heard that," Henry explained to her, "but you are right! Kurt's doing surveillance out of the old recycling plant, and we're hoping to get tape on the Rossi Brothers. We think they're running the recycle plant and have enlisted Jim Thompson to make it look legal and legitimate."

"Can you get me back out there and involved?" Diane pleaded.

"No, not really," he answered, "but I do know somebody that can! If you hang out for a while, I'll text you, then come back to see me. Okay?'

"Oh, thanks Henry, you're the best," she answered. "It's almost lunch; I'll go to the cafeteria and wait for your text."

Diane headed off towards the cafeteria, walking right past the guard. She expected him to say something, but instead all he did was let out a sheepish smile. Perhaps the wife didn't care much for the plan to have the female coworker come home with him for dinner. You think? she answered herself, amused. She sat there waiting, and she expected to see Freddy walk in. He didn't of course and she was glad. Only minutes went by before she got the text. She quickly grabbed two coffees and hurried back to Henry's office. He smiled and thanked her for the coffee.

"You're back in!" he said.

"I am?" she answered.

"Yes!" he replied, "The only prerequisite is that you tell Ms. Winchester what's going on with the Rossi Brothers, and tell her like you're not supposed to be telling her. Can you do that?"

"Sure!" Diane told him, "I'm surprised she doesn't know, but if it'll make it easier to get me back out there, I'll go along with it."

"Okay! Go ahead, go see her!" Henry said, "Unless you want to sit and finish your coffee?"

"Wait, yes, I think I want to do that," she explained. "You've been great help, let's have coffee together."

"Well thank you," Henry smiled, "How has everything else in your life been going?"

"Just perfect," she replied, "In fact, things are going better than ever."

"Does that mean you want to rescind your leave of absence too?" Henry asked.

"Maybe!" she replied, "I guess it depends on how this job goes. Can we just leave it in the air?"

"Sure, Diane," he told her, "I'll just put it in the back of the file."

"And what about you, Henry? What's going on in your life?" she asked, trying to make small talk.

"Oh, not much," he replied, "Nothing much you'd be interested in. Oh wait, I did get a hole in one the other day!"

"A hole in one!" Diane repeated. "Wow! Henry, you should be proud of yourself, that's quite an achievement, a hole in one! Don't you get a reward or a trophy for that sort of thing?"

"I get a plaque with my name on it," he explained.

"Well, you should bring that in and put it on the wall," she directed.

"You think?" he asked.

"Yes, I think you should!" she said, and with that she got up, said goodbye and headed to see Ms. Winchester.

As she made it to Ms. Winchester's door, she went right in. Ms. Winchester had been waving frantically. Not knowing what Diane already knew, she began explaining that someone high up in corporate had called her, telling her to put Diane Wesson to work immediately!

"Somehow, you are back on payroll starting this morning," she explained. "Somehow, they've cut me out of the loop and I don't have to sign or prepare anything? It's out of my hands, so go! Grab your bag at the guard desk, and your instructions and orders are supposed to be in the bag! It seems someone was expecting you. Well? Go!" she ended.

Diane wheeled around and headed for the door. Upon turning the knob, Diane stopped and returned to her chair. She looked at Ms. Winchester solemnly, and explained the story of the Rossi Brothers.

"The recycling plant?" Ms. Winchester asked. "They think the Rossi Brothers are in Hope? Wouldn't that just beat all! That's why you want to get back out there?"

"Yes," Diane answered. "Everyone is very quiet about this operation, it's on a need-to-know basis, I'm sure you understand. I'm not supposed to tell anyone, but I figured you of all people should know."

"Well, thank you very much for telling me. I will remember this, when the time comes, I will recommend you. Now off with you!" she demanded, "Go find Kurt!"

Chapter 11

It All Fits Together

Joe and Ronald spent the entire morning discussing plans and rearranging the shelving and display tables. Except for pauses to take care of customers, they were abustle with excitement. Ideas about where and how to display the projected computers, laptops, tablets, and phones were flying around like crazy!

"Over here!" Ronald said, "They will see the display right when they come in the door!"

"Great idea!" Joe replied, "Where will we display the phones?" They both puzzled on the idea, with neither coming up with a suitable answer. They were debating the pros and cons of having them behind the counter when suddenly Diane walked in.

"What is going on!" Diane exclaimed as she saw the shelves and tables shuffled out of place.

"We're trying to find a spot to display the phones!" Ronald injected, before Joe could even open his mouth.

"Well, at the mall, they are in the main aisle in kiosks!" she instructed, "Why not build a kiosk right here in this corner? It would look great right over there!"

"Perfect!" they both cried out.

"Then it's settled," Joe proclaimed.

"Settled!" agreed Ronald.

"Do you want to help us with the rest?" Joe asked Diane.

"I really can't," Diane explained, "I'm actually working right now! I have to go find Kurt and tell him. I'll be back working with him starting in the morning."

Some customers came in and Diane casually motioned to Joe that she wanted to talk. "I'll be back in a little while," she explained, "and I'm thinking about getting a hotel room to eliminate the travel back and forth, unless maybe, if you want, maybe figure out a way for me to stay here, with you?"

"Here?" Joe pondered, "well, I'd have to fix up some things."

Diane interrupted, "It's okay, I can get a hotel room."

"No," Joe replied, "I'll see what I can do! I'll fix a spot up."

"We'll see," she answered, "see you later then." She smiled at Joe, said goodbye to Ronald and went off to find Kurt.

Joe immediately walked down to the furniture store two blocks away. He picked out a couch that transformed into a day bed. Joe laid down on it and realized that it was far more comfortable than his lumpy cot.

"I'll take it," he told the salesman. He soon had collected an area rug, a nightstand, and a travel alarm. He found some nice room dividers and bought two of them. Somewhat dejected when he found out it couldn't be delivered until tomorrow, he continued anyway and paid in cash. He hurried back to the store before closing time.

"Do you want me to stay over and help straighten these shelves?" Ronald asked.

"Ronald, I can barely pay you regular time, I don't think overtime is in the stars right now," explained Joe.

"Oh, you don't have to worry about that," Ronald explained. "I'd be donating my time for the store! I like working here, I'd be doing it as a friend!"

"Well, isn't that something Ronald, I appreciate that, but no, you go home and get some rest. We have plenty of time to get things arranged. Everything will work out just fine," Joe ranted. "Not just because I'm lucky you know, but because I have some great people around me."

"Aww, shucks!" Ronald mused as he left for home.

Diane got to the spot marked on her instructions. She was at the power company depot. She showed the manager her badge and he called a driver to take her out to the surveillance. That old truck? she thought. She looked up at the bucket raised high into the air, ingenious she thought. She approached the truck and knocked on the side. Suddenly, a part of the truck that looked like a storage compartment cracked open. She peeked into the darkness.

Seeing the familiar LED lights, she whispered, "Kurt?"

The door sprung open and Kurt looked at her and said, "Gee Diane, you scared the crap out of me! What are you doing out here? How the hell did you find me? They said you were on vacation!"

"Easy, Kurt!" she exclaimed, as she entered the truck. Her eyes slowly adjusted and she explained the situation. "I'm going to cut tape for you. I want to finish what we started. Plus, I think you know who the target really is this time."

"You know about that?" Kurt asked, "The Rocci Brothers? It's pretty secret!

Whoever was going to help me wasn't to know until it was absolutely necessary."

"I know," she answered. "But gee Kurt, can't you clean this place up some?"

"Sure, sure, sure, I can have it ready for you by late morning. Will that be soon enough?" he asked.

"I'll be here around nine thirty," she replied. "I have a long drive you know."

"Okay Diane," Kurt was falling all over his words, "It's great, I'm happy, you know, thanks for coming back to help. I'll make it real nice for you." Diane stepped out of the truck, and was driven back to the depot.

Joe was waiting at the door when she pulled up. "I tried," he explained. "They can't deliver anything until tomorrow!"

"That's fine!" Diane said. "I need to go home tonight anyway. I need to get some sweatshirts, jeans, and sneakers. There is no reason to get all dressed up to go work in a dirty old truck. I'll gather up some stuff and plan on staying here the rest of the week."

"Great, that will give me time to get the office straightened around," he told her.

"Sounds like a plan," she replied, as she left.

Diane worried on the ride home, she didn't want to get too close and lose her control, Joe had already done it once by leaning in to kiss her, so she knew she had to be careful. Joe was thinking pretty much the same thing as he lay there before going to sleep.

The next morning, Diane rushed around the apartment collecting all the things she would need for the week. Clothes, makeup, and all her bathroom items were packed and ready. She looked around and grabbed a new bottle of her favorite wine.

Joe's not great at picking wine, she thought, maybe we'll go to a wine tasting experience next weekend? That would be fun! She packed the car, started the motor and backed out of her parking spot. She suddenly opened her door and rushed back into the apartment, leaving the car running and blocking the drive. Once inside, she hurried into the bedroom and carefully placed the item into her purse.

"Can't forget this," she mumbled, and hurried on her way.

Kurt spent the morning cleaning the truck. He swept it all out and put an area rug down on the floor. He wiped down all the electronics and brought in a new computer chair for Diane. I hope she likes it, he worried.

Diane was impressed! As soon as she opened the strange door, she noticed the improvements. "It even smells nice in here," she remarked.

"I hope you're comfy," Kurt responded. There was a small glass bowl full of potpourri on her small desk and next to it was a candle. It wasn't a real candle of course, it was a fake electronic flame in a bulb plugged into the USB port, but it was a nice gesture just the same. They got right down to work, aligning and scanning the recycling yard. Making sure all the cameras were working and focused. This equipment installed in an old truck was even more modern than the van's electronics, there was little to do except watch and wait. Kurt was on his best behavior. He was ecstatic that Diane had requested to join him and he didn't want to screw up. The day went by uneventful, but quickly.

Joe held the door open and motioned the delivery workers to come right in. They brought his purchases into the store, then into the office. Joe had made a large area in the corner for Diane's space. He put down the rug and assembled the table and couch. A small lamp from the recycle plant finished her room. All he needed to do now was position the room dividers he had bought and the job was complete. Nice, he thought, for temporary of course, but she should be comfortable.

When Diane returned to the store, the three of them unloaded the car. Ronald stopped halfway to take care of a customer and Joe showed Diane her new room.

"It's perfect!" she proclaimed, "I just love it."

"I'm glad you like it," Joe said, and proceeded to sit on the couch with her, making certain to keep his distance. "This turns into a bed for night," he explained, "It's quite comfortable."

"I'm sure it will do," she answered.

There was a noise coming from the store and Joe jumped up to investigate. Ronald was still there working on disassembling shelves.

"Why don't you go home, Ronald?" Joe asked, "It's past quitting time!"

"Oh, I know Joe," he replied. "I just want to get this corner emptied out and ready for the kiosk." Joe, realizing his own determination in clearing a corner for Diane, understood why Ronald wanted to finish.

"Okay then," Joe relented, "how can I help?" They discussed Ronald's plan and went to work, giving plenty of time for Diane to settle in.

Diane got ready for bed after positioning all her products in the small bathroom. She looked at the shower and thought, it's small, but it will do! She proceeded to put a sheet onto the transformed bed and grabbed her pillow. She positioned a small blanket to be in reach and lay down on the bed. It felt wonderful. It was like a great weight was lifted from her body and mind. She lay there motionless thinking; this is what it feels like to have a plan come together.

Joe and Ronald finished up with clearing the corner. "We're making good headway," they both agreed.

"Now go home!" Joe teasingly scolded. With that, Ronald left for the night. Joe locked the door and made sure the closed sign was proper. He then went into the office. "You asleep?" he whispered.

"No, not really," she answered, "I'm just enjoying the comfort of this bed you got me."

"I'm so glad you like it," he said. Joe readied himself for bed and proceeded to lie down. It's going to be hard to sleep knowing she's so close, he thought, but he was wrong and drifted right to sleep. It was Diane that couldn't sleep, the strange room and noises along with a feeling of something missing kept her awake. As she lay there she suddenly remembered!

"Joe? Are you asleep?"

"No!" he lied.

"Will you bring me my purse?" she asked.

"Sure," he replied, "where is it?"

"In the bathroom," she muttered. "I think it's in the bathroom." Joe got up and found her purse. He took it to her, announcing himself as he entered.

"Here it is," he told her. "Are you okay?"

"Yes, I'm okay now, I just forgot something," she smiled. She looked magnificent to Joe; he wanted so much to just grab her and squeeze her.

He managed to keep his composure and replied, "Get some sleep, morning comes early." and returned to his cot.

Diane reached into her purse and placed the music box on the small table next to the alarm.

Diane lay there thinking that the music box would allow her to fall asleep. She reached over and lifted the lid. The music box played quietly and she realized that it would not bother Joe, so she reached over and closed then lifted the lid again, as it was playing, she held it and was moving it towards her chest when she dropped it. The music stopped mid note.

Diane frantically reached around the floor for the box. When she found it, she repeatedly opened and closed the lid to no avail. She had broken the one thing she could touch uniting her with Joe. She was heartbroken. She lay there quietly for a long while before deciding to get up.

Joe was sleeping peacefully when Diane whispered, "Joe. Wake up please. Joe, can you wake up for me?" she said louder. Joe started to stir and opened his eyes. It was a beautiful sight to waken to, she looked like an angel in her nightgown, shimmering in the moonlight from the window.

"What do you want?" he asked, realizing he sounded differently than he had hoped and a big smile filled his face.

"I can't sleep," she explained. "I broke my music box!" she whimpered. "Will you fix it for me?"

"Of course, love," he answered. He realized that it was the first time he used that word for her but it fit at that moment.

"Here!" she handed the music box to him. He lay there fumbling with it until he felt the small screw on the bottom. He held his finger to it then handed it back. "There you go," he said with a huge grin. Diane opened the box, but it did not play. She tried again and again without any success. "Joe, will you try again, you didn't fix it," she pleaded. Joe sat up on the edge of the bed and again touched the screw. The blue spark was faint but when he opened the lid, the music box sprung to life.

Diane was overjoyed. "Good night!" Joe told her, and lay back down. Diane quickly went back to her room but as she sat the music box onto the table, she had a thought. She went back into the office and found a laptop on the bench.

"What's up now?" he asked.

"Quiet!" she answered.

"Here! Fix this laptop." she demanded.

"Now?" Joe asked.

"Yes, now!" she replied. Joe started to get up, but she stopped him. "You don't have to get up," she instructed, "just fix it while you're in bed please." Joe held the laptop firmly then handed it back to her. "It's not fixed Joe!" Diane explained as she examined it. Joe sat up and said, "Here, give it back to me." He held the laptop, then once again, handed it back to her. It whirred and clicked and came on. "Perfect." she spoke. "Go back to bed." Joe lay back down wondering if this was going to be how it was going to be. Her waking him at all hours to fix something, but that was definitely not her plan, that was not her plan at all. Diane laid down on her bed. Her mind was racing. Could she be right? Surely, she wouldn't be able to sleep now, she thought. It's time! she thought. I can fix this!

"Joe! Can you come here?" she called out, "Joe?"

"Yes, love!" Joe answered. Joe once again got up from his cot and plodded into her room. "What's wrong, love?" he asked, "are you scared, are you lonely or do you just need tucked in?"

"Yes!" she answered. "All those things and more!" she said, as she grabbed his hand and pulled him gently onto her and into the bed. Joe didn't struggle, he collapsed into her arms and into her lips. They kissed and kissed. During their kiss she managed to get his pajamas off. They clung together and the feeling of his skin touching hers from head to his feet was the most breathtaking and sensual feeling she had ever had. They caressed and explored and finally made love. It didn't end there; within minutes they were kissing again. Over and over, all throughout the night, their bodies joined and became one. The explosions throughout the night from their lovemaking filled the room, and it wasn't until sunrise did the music start to die down.

"I think we just christened this couch," he chuckled.

"You think?" she happily replied. Joe drifted off to sleep, but Diane was not thinking sleep at all anymore. She got up, took a shower, put on her makeup and dried her hair. I'm not angry at all, she decided. In fact, quite the opposite is true! I love him more than ever. She finished up and headed to work throwing him a kiss as he slept.

Chapter 12

Commotion

Joe woke up around ten thirty, and quickly dressed. He went into the store and found Ronald working as usual. He had two customers and he seemed to be taking care of both at once. "Need help?" Joe asked.

"Nope, I have it under control," Ronald replied. The customers seemed to agree, so Joe went back into the office and started fixing computers. There were plenty, and Joe spent the rest of the morning and most of the afternoon getting caught up. Ronald would come back and forth, bringing new electronics to fix, moving the fixed items to the 'done' table and taking those out to waiting customers. On one of those trips Ronald mentioned the customers were inquiring about the new Grand Opening.

"How do customers know about the changes?" Joe asked.

"Oh, I guess I told them and I put it on a flyer stapled outside on the plywood," Ronald explained. "I'm excited about it and I guess the customers are too!"

Joe decided to take a break and look more closely at the outside of the store. Sure enough, there were flyers that Ronald had been putting up, but Joe realized that other bills were also posted there. It was an eclectic assortment and even included a lost cat. While he was perusing the posters, he got a phone call from the workers explaining they were going to replace the windows this afternoon. "Good!" he told them. He now knew that he didn't have to make any decisions about the posters, they'll all be gone soon.

It wasn't long before the truck pulled up, the workers got out and started working. Less than an hour later they were done. Joe offered to take care of the cleanup and Ronald signed the papers. After that they were gone. "It looks great in here, don't you think?" Joe exclaimed.

"Yes, nice and bright again," Ronald remarked, "we'll be ready soon."

Diane got to the truck early, but was surprised to find Kurt already there. Kurt told her he was always early. She settled in for a long boring day. She was watching the camera in the tree and had to continually adjust and focus it. It was windy and she worried that it might blow right out of the tree. Kurt wasn't sure because he didn't install it. Instead, he had paid a neighbor kid to come out with him and his dad one day, to climb the tree.

"He really wants to!" the father said. "Fifty bucks to climb a tree was so important to him that I couldn't tell him no!"
"Well, it's an easy tree to climb," Kurt remarked, "and it's not that high. I'd do it myself if I was younger and my back was a hundred percent again. It's okay, look, he's on his way back down already." Once down, Joe grilled him about whether it was pointing towards the building.

"Yup!" the youngster answered. "I used a whole lot of tape too!"

"Great!" Kurt replied. He handed the boy a fifty-dollar bill and drove them back home.

"He said he used a lot of tape," Kurt explained. Diane was still worried because if someone found a camera lying on the ground, they would become suspicious and the whole investigation could be ruined.

It didn't fall off. The wind died down and Diane just started to breathe easier when Kurt barked, "Something's going on!" Diane focused and indeed the guys were all running around. Some of them ran into the garage area, but this time they took their truck into the garage. They watched intently as the truck backed out, more guys jumped in, and they took off with a huge package tied to the bed of the truck. They left and it was as quiet as normal.

"You get all that?" she asked.

"Sure did!" he answered. "That looked like something important was going down!"

"Indeed," she answered. The truck returned about two hours later without the package. Everything seemed normal again and Diane surmised that they couldn't have gone far, unloaded that package and returned so fast. Maybe the Rocci Brothers were staying in Hope? Maybe they were nearby?

The rest of the day was uneventful and soon Diane and Kurt packed up for the day. "See you tomorrow?" Kurt asked.

"Sure thing," she replied. "I wouldn't miss it for the world," she lied with a laugh. Upon returning to the store, she immediately noticed the new windows. Ronald was closing for the day and held the door for her. "Looks good!" she told him.

"Yeah, and it only took those four guys in their truck about an hour to fix," Ronald explained.

"Four guys and a truck fixed this? This afternoon?" she asked.

"Yup, in and out," he answered. "Well shit!" she said aloud.

Ronald giggled, "Is something wrong?" he asked with a smile.

"No, sorry about that," she said shyly. "I just figured something out."

Diane went into the office. Joe jumped up and bolted towards her, arms open. "Stop!" Diane commanded, "Wait, let's not get ahead of ourselves."

"Are you angry?" he asked.

"No, not at all, that's my point," she explained, "I got up this morning feeling great, your blue spark has no effect when you are laying down! Don't rush over here to hug me, wait until Ronald goes home and I'll meet you on my couch!"

"Holy cow!" Joe exclaimed. "You figured that out last night? I was too sleepy to understand why you were having me fix things in the middle of the night." "That's okay," she said, and proceeded to go into the store to shoo Ronald out for the night.

Diane noticed how much nicer the store was beginning to look, and went into the office to see Joe. She went through the opening between the two dividers and saw Joe, laying there completely naked on her bed.

"I didn't mean that!" she laughed, as Joe quickly covered himself up. She laid down beside him still laughing, and they hugged and kissed. Soon enough they were making love again. Afterwards she asked, "Are you thirsty?"

"Parched!" he replied.

She got up and brought back two big glasses of water and a package of cookies. They lay there cuddling and snacking, talking about the future. It wasn't long before Diane passed out from exhaustion. Joe remained motionless for a long time, watching her breathe. He then carefully reached over her and opened the music box. He thought he noticed a faint smile, and he fell asleep with her as the music was playing.

A Touch of Love

Chapter 13

The Fixer

The rest of the week went by without any excitement. Kurt and Diane had settled into a routine, and so had Joe and Diane. Diane preferred the latter.

It was Friday, right after work, on her way to the store that Diane received the call. She pulled over to the side of the dirt road and dug her phone from her purse.

"Hello?" she said answering the phone.

"The Fixer," was the only reply.

"Are you going to fix Joe?" she squealed.

"Meet me with the subject at 2105 Kirsh Street, in front of the liquor store," the mechanical voice directed. "A large white truck. One hour from now. Don't be late." With that, the phone went click.

"Wait!" Diane tried to question the voice to no avail. Well, that's okay, she thought, we'll just go look for a white truck. Maybe I should stop and see if they have any good wine there? She also realized that she had to change and get ready. I don't want the fixer to see me looking like this, she realized.

At the store she hurried inside and gave Joe the news. "Is there a procedure we must follow?" Joe asked. "Will I get a driver's license?"

"Wait," Diane stopped him, "we just have to go and find out. I'm sure you can ask all those questions to the fixer. I must get ready, you too!" she ordered.

"What?" he answered, "I am ready!"

"Sure!" she replied as she scurried off towards the bathroom. Joe was indeed ready. He wasn't normal. He never put on airs or tried to be someone that he wasn't. Not even play-acting. Joe was always genuine.

She dressed and did her hair in record time, fixed her lipstick and rushed to the car. "Come on!" she yelled back to him as he was giving Ronald last-minute instructions. They had been staying open until nine o'clock on Fridays hoping to increase the weekend business, Ronald had volunteered to work four hours on Saturday for free.

"Don't wait for us if we are late," he hurriedly explained. "Come in tomorrow for a while if you wish, but remember that you don't have to!" With that he hurried to the car. They both knew where the liquor store was, and Diane drove quickly, hoping not to get stopped by the police. She pulled in and parked and checked her phone for the time. Five fifty-eight, she announced. They quickly walked over and motioned to the man driving the big white truck.

"I don't know anything," he blurted before they could speak, "I just drive the truck!"

"What do we do?" she asked him.

"Go over to the side door. It'll either open or it won't. Not up to me, that's all I can say!"

"Thanks!" Joe said and they went over to the side of the truck. The door opened automatically, and they peered inside.

"Come in," a mechanical voice ordered. Diane stepped in first, and explained back to Joe that this was normal, thinking about Kurt's truck. With that vague explanation Joe also stepped inside as the door closed automatically behind him. Spooky, he thought. There wasn't anyone else in the van. Joe glanced around looking for a place that someone could hide, but it quickly became apparent that they were indeed alone. "Sit down and buckle your seatbelts," the voice boomed. Joe and Diane quickly complied. They sat there and realized the truck had started to move. After jostling a bit, the bumping started to smooth out and a computer screen, angled in the corner of the room, suddenly lit brightly. It blinked a few times and then displayed 'The Fixer'. Under the words, a graph-like line similar to a sound mixer appeared every time the voice spoke.

"It has been determined that you are to be fixed," the voice boomed. "You have been given a new name and history. Starting right now, you must embrace this new life and never look back." There was a pause, and then the voice continued. "You will be given a series of instructions that you must follow explicitly. Do you understand?"

"Yes," Joe replied quietly.

"You will also be given a copy of those instructions, and you must dispose of them promptly upon completion of this transformation. The approved method of destruction is to tear the paper into four pieces and burn each one separately in a stainless-steel sink. Will you comply?" Joe answered yes once again.

"Pick up the empty folder on the desk," it beamed, "and place this inside." Joe reached for the binder as a machine that looked like a huge printer spit out a document.

"Memorize these details," it said, as he looked over the birth certificate. All he could read was Joseph Allen Smith when the voice boomed again and the machine spewed out a driver's license, again, Joseph Allen Smith and his picture. Joe didn't have time to recall when he had the photo taken before the voice boomed again.

"Here is your new family history." Joe retrieved a genealogy chart from the machine.

"This is your Social Security card and your work history," the voice continued. "Here are your Visa credit card and your Bank of Hope checkbook. Your account has been approved with your signature and it contains $2000 dollars. Go inside in person, as often as you can, to establish people that can recognize you."

"Next," the voice commanded, and the machine spewed out a concealed pistol license. "Do not go off and buy a gun right away!" it instructed. "Wait for a while until you settle in with your new identity before making any bold moves. This is mostly to show that you have been vetted by the Police Department and are free from any past altercations. On the off chance someone questions your identity, this should end the discussion."

Joe thanked the fixer and shuffled all the papers into the folder.

"Last, we have your instructions and your agreement." Joe glanced over these last papers, noticing the agreement was already signed. A small door popped open and a tray extended. On the tray was a set of keys.

Joe reached out and picked them up quizzically, "Keys?" he asked. He looked at his agreement again and it seemed to be to purchase a truck.

"You have been gifted a 2020 Chevrolet pickup truck." The voice again instructed. "You have two payments left. Do not be late with the payments and be sure to go in and pay in person. Do you understand and agree to this transformation, forever keeping it secret?"

"I do!" Joe agreed. As suddenly as it came on, the screen went black.

They felt the truck come to a stop and the door opened, they stepped out into the dying light of the day, and as their eyes started to adjust, they both realized they were not in Hope anymore.

"Where are we?" she asked quizzically.

"I don't know!" he answered.

They both turned and watched as the driver walked around the front of the truck and climbed up into the passenger side. They heard both doors of the truck slam shut. The truck drove away exposing Diane's car sitting on the side of the road pointed in the opposite direction. The motor was running and keys dangled from the dash. Diane puzzled, immediately reached into her purse and found her keys. Diane went around the car, opened the passenger door and got in, "You drive," she barked, "and keep the keys. Seems like I already have my set!"

Joe drove towards some electric lines in the distance. They must want us to go this way, he decided. When they got closer, he recognized the road, "State Road," he said, "not far from the recycling plant." He turned towards Hope.

Diane quizzed him, "Are you happy now?"

"It hasn't sunk in," he told her. "But yes, this is a great feeling after not knowing all this time. I now have papers that explain exactly who I am. What could beat that?"

As they drove back to Hope, Diane looked over the papers. "How can you not remember anything but remember how to drive so well?" she asked, still flipping through all Joe's new papers.

"I'm not sure, I just know how, I guess. It must be like riding a bike, you don't forget! I guess I can ride a bike too!" he laughed.

She continued to look through the papers and read something interesting. "Hey!" she exclaimed. "Your new truck."

"Yes, what about it?" Joe asked.

"It's at the same place!" she told him.

"The same place? You mean the liquor store?" he asked.

"According to this, it's the same address," she told him.

Sure enough, upon arriving back to the parking lot, a shiny blue Chevy pickup was sitting in the same place that they had left Diane's car. Diane pressed the key fob and the taillights blinked and the truck chirped. She handed him the keys and exuberantly said, "Your chariot awaits you! Wow!" Joe thought, better than I

could have ever hoped for. My lucky
streak continues.

Chapter 14

The Blue Spark

Diane motioned him to follow her into the store. Joe was surprised to see how bright and clean this store was. "The State runs this store," she explained, "they are always like this. Don't ever go into one of the dingy liquor stores you might find in the big cities. They can be a mess, but this one is safe. There are many safety features and the crooks know all about them. There are cameras and the police are automatically called, plus the front door locks as soon as the crook tries to get out, the bulletproof glass comes up and traps him, only to wait for the police." Joe noticed the cracks in the floor protecting every aisle.

Amazed, he asked her, "How do you know all this?"

"I'm in the business," she lied. She really knew this from a clerk at the local store just like this one, close by her apartment. She always went there and recognized this store to be the same. "Over here!" Diane motioned to Joe. "Look here!" she showed him. "This is Chardonnay. Notice the wine is clear. It's a white wine, it can even be yellow. We are looking for pink."

"Down there!" Joe pointed.

"Ahh yes, Chardonnay Rose," Diane exclaimed. "That's it. It's very hard to find sometimes."

"It's very expensive too," Joe mentioned.

"But it's also very good," Diane explained, as she took it and partially skipped to the cashier.

"I'll pay for that!" he said, as he caught up to her.

"Nope," she replied, "you can't, honey. They don't take cash here anymore. Cuts down on crime! There is no money to steal!"

Wonderful, he thought, remembering that she had not given him his new credit card, and noting that she called him honey. Honey, he bemused himself, I like honey. They left the store and both got into their respective vehicles.

"Meet you at the store!" That was the last thing she said to him.

They partially raced to the store. At the light, Joe pulled up beside her and revved his new engine. Diane just flipped her hair at him and when the light turned, she rocketed off leaving the truck in the dust. "You win this time!" he said out loud. "The Fixer told me to lay low, so I'm just following orders!" When they arrived, Diane was laughing at him, but Joe was noticing all the people in the store. It was like a party going on. Joe read the flyers saying it was a Pre-Grand Re-Opening sale. Free coffee, doughnuts and sodas. Get 10% off, the flyer said.

When Joe entered the store, he was overwhelmed about the music playing and the party atmosphere. Everyone was really enjoying themselves, talking and dancing. Ronald had placed signs and pictures of all the products Joe had picked out but hadn't yet ordered. Each one was in its respective display. He even had a big sign that said "PHONES" where the kiosk was going to be. Each display had a box full of tickets saying ten percent off, and followed by the respective product. It was brilliant! As Joe looked around, Diane approached him from the rear.

"Look!" she spoke. "There's the construction worker that had you fix his laptop. Go talk to him," she prodded. She quickly followed up with "Don't touch him, honey!"

"I won't!" he quipped back. Joe approached the worker and said, "Good to see you again!" The worker thrust out his hand to shake but Joe quickly said, "Sorry, I spilled some soda!" and he pretended to wipe it on his pants. "It's real sticky still," he said.

"That's okay," the worker said. He gave no indication that he had ever been mad at Joe. "Hey, that laptop has worked perfectly since you fixed it for me, but I'm looking at getting a new computer next week," he explained.

"What's the problem?" Joe asked.

"Well," the worker continued, "I'll be needing a phone soon too, and one for my daughter. Can I take one of each coupon, and maybe two for the phones?"

Joe let out a huge smile. "Take two of each if you like, my good friend! Repeat customers are our favorite around here. Especially happy customers! Enjoy your coffee, grab a doughnut, grab an extra doughnut and take it to your daughter. Tell her I'll be waiting for her arrival!"

"I knew I liked you," he replied, as he gathered up the discount tickets.

Joe approached Ronald for the first time since getting back.

"What do you think, boss?" Ronald asked.

"You did good!" Joe answered, "I'm truly impressed."

"I've been planning this and checking out your order forms," Ronald explained. "I've been praying you liked the idea.

You've been so busy I figured I'd surprise you."

As the party died down, Joe turned off the music and ushered people out the door. He sent Ronald home, flipping the sign to closed. Diane had vanished for the last half hour and Joe hurriedly went to the office to find her. He found her sitting at the desk with a half full glass of wine in her hand; he noticed the bottle half empty.

"What?" he asked. "Only one glass?"

"This bottle is not for you," she advised. "This is part of my plan."

"What's the plan?" Joe asked.

"You'll see as soon as I get my courage up," Diane replied. "The plan is for me to touch you." She tossed him the alarm clock from the table. "Keep track of the time, I will want to know how long I'm mad at you." She walked over to him and gulped down the last of the wine in her glass. She reached out her finger. She quickly pulled back her hand and went to sit at the desk. Pouring herself another glass of wine, she again approached him, quite tipsy now. Joe thought this game was fun, but the look on Diane's face reminded him that it was serious. She reached out and touched his cheek, the blue spark encircled her hand.

"Nothing!" she shouted, "nothing at all, I feel great! I'm immune, the wine makes me immune." She was laughing as she let go. "Why did you do that?" she shouted, "what the hell is wrong with you, why would you do something like that?"

"What did I do?" he asked.

"You're making me feel bad!" she cried, "I feel horrible, why would you do that?" She was crying as she ran to her room. I don't think she's immune, Joe thought. I don't think the wine helped. He stared at the clock for what seemed like hours. Soon she peeked her head around the corner of the divider and sheepishly asked, "Are you mad at me?"

"Me mad at you?" Joe answered. "Certainly not," he cried. "Are you still mad at me? That's the real question."

"No," she said, "I realize it's the touch and the blue spark that ticked off. I guess I'm not immune," she decided. She realized that the wine did help, so she walked over and poured herself another glass. "The time was five minutes, almost six," Joe explained. I guess that wasn't too bad, she realized, it could have lasted an hour or even more; five minutes isn't bad, she thought, I can work with that.

She reached out to touch him again, pausing just long enough for him to ask, "Are you sure you want to do this?"

"Yes, I'm sure," she replied and touched his arm. Once again, the blue spark encapsulated her finger and she explained how good she felt. The entire time she had touched him, she felt great; no, not great, better than great. As she held her finger to his arm, she realized that it wasn't the touch that made her angry, that it was when she quit touching him, that's when she would get mad. She had this thought prepared in her mind as she let go, hoping she could control her anger. "Damn you!" she said, "damn it all, Joe, what the hell are you doing! I really wouldn't think you'd do that to me again! Just what the hell is wrong with you?" she cried.

"I'm sorry," he answered, "I'm very sorry."

"It's all your fault!" she yelled and went crying to her room again. Joe wanted to follow her but held his ground. Again, he stared at the clock ticking away in his lap. He started looking for her to come back at five minutes and sure enough she did.

Sheepishly she approached him, "Sorry," she said softly, "lie down, you big lug, I'm done for the night." He laid down on the cot, and she lay next to him. "Honey," she asked, "do you think we will ever figure it out?"

"Oh, you'll figure it out," he answered, "and knowing you, it will be soon." He laid there thinking as she fell asleep. Not long went by, and Joe got up, lifted her up in his arms, and carried her off to her bed in her room. He put her on the bed and lay down beside her. It was far more comfortable than his small lumpy cot. She once again fell asleep in his arms.

A Touch of Love

Chapter 15

Wine Tasting Experience

When Joe woke up the next morning, he quietly got out of bed and decided to let her sleep. He got dressed and went out to the store area. Ronald was already there. He helped Ronald clean up from the night before, and prepare for today. Ronald busily adjusted the posters and added 10% discount coupons to the boxes. Joe turned on the music and set out some sodas and donuts that Ronald had brought. The last thing he did in preparation was start the coffee. Customers came in, chatted, and picked up the coupons. It was not a party like Friday night but everyone seemed to enjoy themselves. Joe could not get over the fact that Ronald had planned all this by himself. Diane came out and joined them around 10:30. She seemed none the worse from her ordeal last evening. Chipper and cheerful, she reminded him that she had made a reservation for a wine tasting on Sunday.

"You feel you will be ready by then to enjoy wine?" Joe asked.

"I feel fine," she said. "The reason I slept in was probably more your fault." She laughed.

"I knew you'd blame me," he said jokingly. After the sale ended and Ronald went home, their day was quiet. Joe asked Diane if she wanted to walk down to the supermarket with him. She declined but gave him a list of things to pick up.

He very much wanted to drive his truck, but relented as it was just a block and a half and he never minded the walk in the past. Once there, he gathered the stuff on the list and walked over to the meat department. He chose two very nice ribeye steaks, but again he put them back, this time choosing two larger porterhouse steaks instead. A slight smile formed on his face. He took the groceries, waiting in line for his favorite cashier. As his turn came, he put the items on the belt and said "Hello."

She looked up at him, smiled and said, "By the way, Joe, rumor has it that next month we will stop taking and handling cash, altogether." Joe smiled and handed her his credit card. She looked the card over and smiled again. "So, your name really is Joe Smith. Well, I'll be, I always thought you to be an undercover spy or something like that, with a fake name." She laughed as she packed his groceries.

Joe smiled at her and replied, "No, I'm just a regular guy like everyone else," and proceeded to walk home.

That evening, Joe continued to work on the computers, phones and a laptop, while Diane dusted and vacuumed to tidy the place up. She considered going home for the night but would have to come back to get Joe for the wine tasting experience. She had the clothes so she decided to stay the night again.

Sunday morning came and went, and they prepared to go to the wine tasting. Joe put on his best suit, and Diane was dressed to kill. They went outside and Joe motioned for her to get in the truck.

"We should take my car," she said, and reluctantly he agreed.

"Well, I do have my own set of keys," he declared as he got in the driver's seat. He put the top down, and drove to the vineyard near the edge of town. Upon arriving they joined a large group of couples, waiting for the steward. He took them to a room and poured a red wine into the glasses for everyone. Joe had watched a video on wine tasting but that was his only knowledge. He swirled, sniffed, and took a sip, swished it in his mouth and swallowed. Delightful, he thought.

Diane whispered to him, "Plain, but okay for a start," she said. Joe just smiled. The tour went through the distillery, and they stopped at nooks along the way, tasting and discussing the wines. Almost finished, they were led outside and directed towards the vineyard to a small set of tables. It was a beautiful day and Diane was having a wonderful time; she was also hoping Joe was enjoying himself. They walked single file towards the tables. Halfway there, Diane's heel sunk into the ground and she lost her balance. Joe instantly caught her before she fell. She smiled at him but both realized that they had to hold hands for the rest of the experience. He held her hand, and looked ahead. Between him and the tables was a small creek. The bridge was designed for one person at a time, and it had ropes for balance on both sides. Joe stopped in his tracks.

"Lay down on the ground!" he demanded of her.

"What?" she replied, "here?"

"Lay down on the ground right now!" he demanded again. She sat down first then lay down in the nice grass. Everyone in the group was shocked. With everyone looking, Joe proceeded to lay down beside her and give her a kiss. "Will someone take a picture of us?" he asked. Almost everyone gathered around and took pictures with their phones. The mood lightened and everyone laughed as a stranger took Diane's hand and helped her up. Joe got up by himself and motioned for her to go past him.

"After you, my love," he spoke, and she approached the bridge. He heard the couple behind him talking.

"Why don't you ever do anything romantic like that with me?" the wife said to her sheepish husband.

They ate bread, cheese and crackers at the tables and finished the tour.

They sang and laughed on the way back to the store. Once there, Diane explained that she had to go home and get more clothes.

"Talk to you Monday after work?" she asked.

"I'll be looking forward to it very much!" he explained. "I'll miss you terribly."

"I'll miss you too," she admitted. She blew him a kiss, and left for her apartment.

Joe had plenty to do. He finished the order for the computers, laptops, tablets and phones. He located the folder and retrieved the credit card. He typed in the information. He checked the overnight delivery box on two of each of the items. He electronically signed at the bottom of the order for the credit on the entire order and monthly payments. Finally, he said to himself, a real store. He then proceeded to call a carpenter to build the kiosk.

"Do you have plans for the job?" the carpenter asked.

"No," Joe replied, "just use your own judgment, we want one similar to the ones in the mall."

"Well, I got you," he replied. "I can be there tomorrow afternoon?"

"That would be wonderful!" Joe answered, and the deal was struck. Joe proceeded to memorize everything The

Fixer had given him. He soon knew everything about himself. He took the paper with the instructions, ripped it into four pieces and went into the bathroom, burning them in the sink one at a time. With that done, he took the time to daydream. Everything is really going well, he thought. If we can just figure out how to control the blue spark, it would be perfect. I could even ask Diane, oh well, I shouldn't get ahead of myself, he muttered.

Diane had the time to daydream too. He said it, she thought to herself, he said it out loud, I know I heard him. He said it in the liquor store, loud and clear. I just have to get him to say it again. "I'm allowed to daydream!" she said out loud.

A Touch of Love

Chapter 16

I Can Fix This

Monday morning, Joe met Ronald at the door. He explained to Ronald that if they got a delivery today, it would mean the entire order had been accepted and would be following soon. "Great news!" Ronald exclaimed. Joe also explained that the carpenter was coming this afternoon to build the kiosk. "You are really moving things forward, boss," Ronald said happily.

Joe helped Ronald get started for the week, then jumped into his truck and drove off to make a payment on his truck. While there, he sat down with the manager and filled out all the paperwork for a business loan.

"Everything looks good!" the manager told him. "I'll run it past corporate, but I'm sure it will be accepted! I'll call you as soon as I know!" he explained. As the manager reached out his hand, Joe looked down at his shoes, pretending not to notice. He brushed an imaginary blemish off and wheeled around as he got up. Joe quickly gave the manager the thumbs up sign and the manager repeated it right back as Joe left the store.

Joe moved on to the bank. He sat with the manager talking for a long time. He filled out some forms, and the manager went and brought him some packages. Joe had his hands full while getting up and nodded and thanked him as he left.

When Joe returned to the store, Ronald was ecstatic! "It arrived!" Ronald proclaimed. "I'm setting things up now."

In between customers, Ronald was unboxing and displaying the laptops. He had the display with the tablets finished too. He was working on the computers when Joe called him over behind the counter.

"Steady this chair as I climb up on it," Joe asked

"Sure, Boss," Ronald replied. Ronald watched intently, wondering what was up, as Joe revealed a screwdriver and proceeded to pry the Cash Only sign off the wall.

"Hurray!" Ronald cried out. Joe replaced it with a Visa/Mastercard placard and climbed down. He gave Ronald some posters and stickers to apply around the store and proceeded to go outside and place a clear-backed sign on the glass door. Perfect, he thought. Ronald was opening the packages he had brought from the bank, and the two of them installed the new card reader to the cash register.

The carpenter showed up and both Joe and Ronald carried wood into the store, stacking it close to where the kiosk was to be built. The carpenter climbed out of his truck loaded with tools. Both the truck and the trailer had signs saying "American Spirit Carpenters" and had a picture of an American flag. I like that, Joe thought. The carpenter's name was Joe also. Ronald took to calling him 'Mister Joe', while calling Joe, 'Boss'.

"It's a kit," Mister Joe explained. "No sawing needed unless of course the engineers made a mistake," he kidded. There were pounding sounds and occasionally a compressor started up, but for the most part, business went on as usual.

Diane arrived at the store and Joe noticed that she seemed tired. She came into the store and marveled at the changes. Her mood changed to perky as she wandered about, pointing out everything and meeting the carpenter. "It's perfect!" she proclaimed.

"It's not finished," he told her, "I have to glue on some gingerbread and make some final touches tomorrow." Everyone thanked him as he left and Joe shooed Ronald home.

Diane held Joe's hand and gave him a kiss. He led her to the office and lay down on the bed as she sat down next to him.

"I'm exhausted," she spoke.

"I can see," he told her.

"I took care of dinner," he explained.

"You did?" she questioned.

"Yes," he told her with a smile, "I ordered us pizza."

"You are wonderful!" she smiled as she got up and went into the bathroom. Joe got up and quickly called the pizza restaurant and ordered their meal. No harm, no foul, he mused.

They ate pizza together and Diane decided to go to bed early. "I'm really tired," she explained.

"You go ahead, Love," Joe told her, "I just need to finish up here." Diane went to her room and to sleep, and Joe heard the music box play and smiled. He worked on fixing the computers quietly. A few hours passed and Joe finished up. He got ready for bed and peered into her room; she was lying there in the dark, naked, covered only by the moonlight through the window. Joe looked at her intently, resisting the temptation to waken her. He returned to his cot longing and wanting her more than anything else he had ever wanted in his life.

The next few days went by quickly. It was Friday and Joe decided to move his truck around to the back of the store. There was a parking area there, and a door for deliveries. Joe wanted to free up space for parking as the store got busier and busier. He noticed a doorbell and pushed it. Finally, Ronald opened the door. "I didn't know what that buzzer noise was at first," Ronald told him. "But I figured it out."

"I'm just glad it works," Joe explained. "We should get this storage room cleaned up. We will be getting deliveries from here on out, and we need a place to store extra supplies and merchandise too!"

"I'll get right on it, Boss!" Ronald said.

Diane returned to the store later than usual that evening. She had spent a lot of time thinking about Joe and the store while she whiled away the hours in the truck. She had an idea and after work, she stopped at the costume shop. Diane stood next to the kiosk and told Ronald to pretend to look at the new phones as if he was a customer. When he got close, Diane opened the bag, put on an apron and proceeded to put on a French beret hat and a bushy fake mustache. "May I help you," she said in a thick French accent. They both laughed out loud.

"You certainly can!" Ronald played along.

"You try it! Joe!" Diane teased.

"I don't—" Joe started to say.

"Please?" Diane pleaded.

"Sure," Joe relented. He put on the apron, hat and mustache, stepped into the kiosk and said, "May I help you," in an attempt at a French accent. Ronald and Diane howled.

"That was great!" they both cried.

"Now you! Ronald," Joe insisted. Not to be outdone, Ronald donned the costume and drawled, "Ma eh elp ewue?" in the best French accent of them all. Everyone laughed. Ronald quickly fashioned a nametag labeled 'Pierre'. "So, it's settled," Ronald continued, "I'll get a bell for the kiosk and whenever someone rings it, one of us, mostly me of course, will put on the costume and become Pierre!"

"It's actually quite brilliant!" Joe exclaimed. "We will have a permanent employee manning the kiosk without hiring anyone new!"

They closed the shop, bid Ronald goodnight, and hurried into the office flirting and kissing all the way to Diane's bed. After they had made passionate love, Joe got up and retrieved some bread, cheese and wine he had prepared. They ate, talked and laughed while sitting up in bed. Every time she brushed against him or they accidentally touched, they would latch hold of each other, lie down, kiss and get back up separately.

Diane kicked Joe out of bed while she put the leftovers away. When she returned Joe had vacuumed up all the crumbs. She undressed in front of him and lay down on the bed.

"Sleep here with me, honey. Will you?" She scrunched over next to the wall and prepared him a spot.

"Of course, love," he answered. He returned to her arms and as they made love again, she opened the music box.

The next morning, Diane explained to Joe that she had to go home for the rest of the weekend. She needed to do laundry, go to the dry cleaners and pick up some necessities. She also informed him that she had to go to headquarters for a special meeting on Monday, but was unsure of its agenda. They kissed, lay down on Joe's cot, kissed again, then she left.

After Diane returned home, she realized how nice she had been living here in this luxurious apartment. I know now I don't need these amenities, she calculated. I would live with a dirt floor with him, she thought. Well, maybe not a dirt floor, but she was sure he was indeed her soulmate. I'm not going to let go of him, she told herself.

The store had indeed been approved for credit by the distributor and Joe had also received the okay on his loan application. The shipments at the store started coming in on Saturday and the store shelves were filling, emptying, and getting restocked. Business was brisk and Joe ordered a large sign to hang outside. It read "Grand Re-Opening."

A Touch of Love

Chapter 17

Friends in High Places

Diane returned to headquarters on Monday morning. She watched her reflection in the mirror-like windows as she walked into the building, and her confidence grew. She walked past the guard desk, casually waving at them again. She went straight to Ms. Winchester's office.

"We are closing down the surveillance!" Ms. Winchester blurted out.

"What?" Diane complained. "You can't stop us now! We haven't got any good tape yet."

"That's the exact reason," Winchester explained. "All the facts point towards Jim Thompson being involved with the Standard Investment Conglomerate, and that's run by the Rocci's. We can prove that he rents the building to Joe Smith, incriminating him. We're going to haul him in and either he turns State's Evidence against the Rocci Brothers or we confiscate the whole Recycling Center and auction it off. That should bring in enough to pay for the investigation."

"I mustn't let that happen. I'm going to go talk to Henry right now," and she stormed out of Ms. Winchester's office. Diane burst into Henry's office and proceeded to tell him what Ms. Winchester had told her.

"I need more time!" she begged.

"Calm down," Henry told her and picked up the phone and dialed. Diane listened as Henry explained the situation to the voice on the phone, "She needs more time!" Henry explained, "Yes, we will wait for his call," and hung up.

"Who was that?" Diane asked.

"Just wait," Henry said.

"Should I get you coffee?" she asked.

"Just wait!" Henry said more sternly. Diane sat there quietly. A few minutes later, the phone rang. "Answer it!" Henry prodded, "It's for you!"

"For me?" she asked as she answered and said, "Hello."

"Please stand by while I connect you to the Vice President of the United States," the voice instructed.

"Diane? Diane Wesson?" the voice asked.

"Yes, I'm Diane Wesson, Mr. Vice President." She was shaking as she answered.

"I'm glad to be able to finally talk to you," he explained, "I've been keeping track of you ever since the Gregory Marlin case, I'm sure you recall that."

"Oh yes!" she replied, "I remember that case."

"Well, Greg was a close friend of my fathers, in college, and he was delighted when he found out it was you that refused to give up on the case and finally proved that it was that Kimber guy who concocted that whole scam. My father wishes to thank you and so do I," the Vice President exclaimed. "I can think of no better way to show my appreciation than to give you more time on this case if that's what you want."

"Oh yes, it is! I need more time on this case!" she cried.

"Well, I'll make a call, but don't worry, carry on, they'll do as I ask."

"Thank you, Mr. Vice President, thank you so much," Diane said happily.

"Good luck," he told her and hung up.

She almost hung up as a computer-generated voice began to speak. "You have just received a call from the Vice President of the United States. All calls are recorded but kept confidential by law. We ask that you keep this call confidential." Half in shock, Diane hung up the phone.

"Did that help?" Henry said as he smiled from ear to ear.

"Oh Henry, you're the best!" Diane exclaimed, as she overly shook his hand. "I could just kiss you!"

"That would be against protocol," he chuckled, "but a quick kiss on the cheek might be a payment for a call from the Vice President of the United States!" Diane indeed kissed Henry on the cheek and pranced out of his office. Diane opened the door to Ms. Winchester's office as she walked by.

"I took care of it!" she said, and left Ms. Winchester with the oddest, quizzical look on her face. Diane returned home, packed the things she needed for the coming week. I'll explain everything to Kurt tomorrow, she thought.

Chapter 18

Touchdown

Diane spent Tuesday morning explaining everything to Kurt. It was funny because she had started out by telling him as soon as she climbed into the truck that she was friends with the Vice President of the United States! That had gotten his attention. They soon settled in to another boring day. Nothing unusual had happened all day. Diane took the time during the lull to compliment Kurt for his new attitude and his lack of crudeness that he used to display.

"I like the new Kurt," she told him.

"Well, I kind of found someone I like," he told her.

"Tell me all about it," Diane probed.

"Well, they hired a new girl to cut tape and are training her, but she came to see me about coaching her after work." Kurt explained. "We've been working together and I've been helping her ever since. Over the weekend, she told me she likes me! I'm really starting to fall for her Diane!"

"Well good for you, Kurt. My advice is to just keep being the Kurt you have been since I've come back to work with you, and you'll do fine," while Diane was giving him advice, Kurt noticed a commotion.

"Look!" he spoke.

They peered through the cameras, making sure all were working and watching the commotion. The workers were running around and cleaning up frantically. "They are cleaning up outside the gate," Diane reported. The magnet crane was picking up all the metal that was strewn around the yard.

"Two guys are raking the ground and one is sweeping, something big is up," Kurt said.

"I hope so!" She replied.

They went on like this for around two hours, running everywhere they went, and Kurt pointed out the big circle they were slowly painting on the ground. They watched as one guy with a phone walked around and every so often pointed at the ground. Another worker painted a line where he had pointed. They continued as it formed an oval painted on the ground.

"Odd," Diane said.

"No, not odd at all," Kurt explained, "that's the area that the security camera can detect. I think whatever is about to happen, will happen in the circle!"

"You're right!" Diane agreed, "Perhaps not in it though," she argued, "perhaps the opposite is true?"

"Interesting," Kurt replied.

They watched intently. Soon it all quieted down. It had gone past quitting time but neither one moved an inch. They waited. An hour passed; Kurt started squirming in his chair.

"I know," Diane answered, even though he hadn't said a word. Suddenly a worker came out and opened the gate. A black car with the windows tinted pulled up. Kurt held his breath as he rechecked all the cameras and checked the tapes. Diane was focused on the car, when another black car, very similar to the first, pulled up and parked. A man got out of the back seat of both vehicles and they proceeded into the yard surrounded by bodyguards.

"It's the Rocci's!" Diane squealed. "Shh," Kurt motioned.

Everyone was in the office area, when four guys came out and opened the trunk of the second black car. It took three of the men to get the package out of the trunk, the fourth looked around, seeming to be a lookout. They brought a junk car over to the crusher and placed the package inside.

"Is that a body?" Diane asked.

"Can't be sure," he answered.

A worker was scampering up the magnet crane ladder, and soon it lifted the car into the crusher. Everyone had come out of the office and were watching as the lid crashed down onto the car. Over and over, it crashed until the hydraulic motors started to further crush the car. It didn't take long before the car was reduced to a small cube. The magnet crane picked it up and placed it on the pile with the others.

"Did we get it?" Diane asked, shaking.

"We got it," Kurt assured her.

"Are you positive?" she asked again.

"I'm positive!" he said with a big grin.

Diane quickly dialed 911. "I want to report a possible murder!" she said. "I'm doing surveillance for the IRS and we believe we've filmed a body getting disposed of, in a car crusher, out at the recycling plant," she explained. She was on the phone with the operator when Kurt called for a driver to come drive the truck. Kurt then pulled and meticulously time and dated the tapes. He marked "touchdown" on all the tapes involved. After a short wait, a driver came and lowered the bucket and drove back to the parking area, seemingly unaware of the passengers or the content.

During the ride, Diane looked directly at Kurt and said, "We got the Rocci Brothers!"

As they were getting ready to leave, Diane asked Kurt if he could find and bring his new girlfriend.

"Sure," he replied.

"Well, get her and bring her to my apartment, okay?" She explained. "She should get her name on this, and get off to a good start at the department. We'll make sure your name is on this cut in big letters too! If you want, meet us at the computer store and you can follow me. You know where that is, right?"

"Well, I better," he laughed, "did you forget that this all started there?" Diane laughed, feeling stupid, and left to pick up Joe.

"Where have you been?" Joe asked.

"We got the Rocci Brothers!" she shouted.

"Great news!" he spoke.

"Did you clear Jimbo?"

"Not yet, but these tapes should do the trick," she explained. "Get ready and come to my apartment tonight, Kurt and his girlfriend are coming too, she's taking my place, oh never mind, I'll tell you everything on the way."

Joe readied himself and put the top up on the car while waiting. Soon Kurt pulled up and honked, Joe waved to him and took off for Diane's with Kurt in tow. She explained the whole story to him with him barely saying more than, 'Go on!'

Once there, Diane welcomed everyone in, meeting Juliana, Kurt's girlfriend, for the first time. Diane opened and poured everyone a glass of Chardonnay Rose. She was distributing them while Kurt moved a kitchen chair next to her workstation and started sorting and piling the tapes. Joe and Juliana stood back, watching as Diane and Kurt worked through the pile. "This cut is easy," she kept remarking, while glancing back at Juliana. "It's not hard once you get the hang of it." Diane cut and pasted the tape together, starting the story with the preparation by the workers, then of the Rocci Brothers getting to the Recycling Plant and was ready to show the body getting unloaded from the trunk when she stopped for a break.

"Another glass of wine?" she asked everyone. Everyone agreed and Diane poured the rest of the bottle. "I have another around here somewhere!" she announced. "If we don't get this done soon, you'll fit in fine around here if you like this wine!" Diane said as she smiled at Juliana. Soon she was back at work, and everyone winced as the lid fell on the crusher the first time. She showed that they never went inside the painted circle, and finished up.

"Everyone here understands that although we call it cutting tape, we don't disturb any original tape. All the tape is in its original form and time date encoded to prove continuity. We merely copy and reproduce to provide an easy-to-follow movie so that everyone can follow and understand the case without having to watch the hours of boring footage that doesn't contain any action, or unrelated footage not important to the case." Diane finished her speech and everyone was smiling. "We are all going to get a raise," she laughed. Everyone clinked their almost empty glasses and Kurt and Juliana packed up the tapes and left for Hope. "It's on you two now," Diane acknowledged, "protect that tape and deliver it to headquarters in the morning." Diane had created two copies of the finished cut. She handed the second tape to Joe. She had cleared Jimbo to the IRS, but they still had the local police to convince. "Take this to the Hope police," she spoke. "This will help clear Jimbo if he's in any trouble."

Jimbo was indeed in trouble, Jimbo was in a heap of trouble, as they had been interrogating him this whole time. They had discovered the dead body but no one else was around when they arrived. They had taken Jimbo in for questioning, hoping to get to the bottom of the crime.

"I can assure you that Jimbo doesn't know anything. I'm Joe Smith, I rent the building owned by the Rocci Brothers, but I didn't know that, Officer Steyr," Joe said, as he read the name tag under his badge. "I didn't know that at all. Wait, I have a tape showing exactly what happened today that will clear Jimbo," and Joe handed the tape to the officer.

"By saying Jimbo, you mean Jim Thompson, right?" the Officer asked.

"Yes!" Joe declared. "His name is Jim Thompson; everybody calls him Jimbo."

"Oh, we know who he is. He's very well liked around here, we just must be formal," the officer explained. "No one gets preferential treatment when there is a crime like this."

"Okay, I understand. Do you know where he is?" Joe asked.

"He's here!" the officer answered. "Under interrogation."

"Can I see him?" Joe asked.

"I don't see why not; we haven't been able to get anything out of him," answered Officer Steyr. "Either he's a real hard nut to crack or he really doesn't know anything about the murder. That officer will take you to him, I'll be along after I watch this tape."

Joe followed the police officer down the hall. He stopped to unlock the door and motioned Joe to go in. Joe saw Jimbo sitting in the corner as the guard closed the door. Jimbo jumped up and grabbed his arm, shaking his hand with the other. Jimbo had his gloves on of course, and he thanked Joe for coming to see him.

"I didn't come to see you, Jimbo," Joe said, "I came to spring you, my old friend."

"Spring me?" Jimbo asked.

"Yes, I said spring you. I brought them a tape Diane made that proves you didn't have anything to do with the murder or the attempted disposal of the body." Joe explained.

"Is that what this is all about?" Jimbo asked.

"Yes," Joe answered. "It seems a lot happened, right under your nose."

"Tell me all about it," Jimbo asked.

"I better not!" Joe answered, "It is probably better that you don't know things right now."

"Well heck, Joe," Jimbo explained. "I never did anything illegal in my life."

"I believe you!" Joe replied, "Now let's get the cops to believe you."

Officer Steyr entered the room. "We seem to have quite a few angles, and clear movies showing everybody involved in the incident today," he explained. "I've studied them quite close, and Mr. Thompson, you don't appear to be in any of the pictures. When was the last time you were near that car crusher?"

"That car crusher on the other side of my lot?" Jimbo asked. "I don't ever go over there, officer, I steer clear of that side, way too dangerous for my blood. I let the guys that rent it handle all the work on that side. Nope, don't go over there, haven't needed to, haven't wanted to."

"So, who do you rent it to?" Officer Steyr asked.

"Oh, that's a strange one," Jimbo started to explain. "I guess I really don't know what his name is, well I do, I just can't remember it, we really don't have a deal on paper. The guys just came over one day and had a proposition."

"And what was the proposition?" he asked.

"Well, they told me they had a building, storefront type building, and they were prepared to trade it to me, for the use of that side of the recycling plant. No paperwork, no lease, no nothing. They just wanted an even trade that lasted until either one of us wanted to quit the deal. After that, we would have three months to move out, and so would they. I never did like going over on that side, and

I knew Joe would really do well if he had his own place, so I had my cousin Walter pretend to rent the store to Joe. It all worked out well till the quake. Joe figured it out because Walter couldn't do anything about the damaged windows. But even after that seemed to be okay until you guys dragged me in here."

"Okay Mr. Thompson," the officer stated, "We're going to cut you loose, we don't have any reason to charge you, we will inform you when you can return to the recycling plant. You can both go now, just don't leave town, got it!"

"Well, I'm not going anywhere," Jimbo said, "except to bed, I'm exhausted," he explained. As Joe and Jimbo were leaving, Officer Steyr explained to Joe that he had to keep the tape.

"Well, that's fine," Joe answered, "I was just going to drop it off anyway. You keep it. I'm told the IRS keeps the raw original files under lock and key. You'll have to see them about getting a hold of those if you want them." And they left.

"Are you okay, Jimbo?" Joe asked.

"I'm fine!" Jimbo answered, "I've been through a lot harder times than them asking me a few questions. It does tire a guy out though; I got to get some rest."

"You want to get something to eat first?" Joe asked.

"Another time," Jimbo answered, "another time." And they each went home.

Joe went to the store and wrote a long note for Ronald. He explained most of the proceedings and that he had Diane's car so that he had to return it to her tonight. He told Ronald in the note not to worry but he didn't know whether he'd be back in hours or in days. He just didn't know what was going to happen. He then started the long drive to Diane's apartment. It was 2:00 a.m. when he got to her house. He woke her and she shuffled him up to her bedroom. He was asleep before he knew he had laid down.

Diane got up early and went to the IRS Corporate Offices. She was amazed when she found out that Kurt and Juliana were already there. They were in the presentation room playing the tape. Diane stepped inside and sat in the back. From there she could see Henry, Ms. Winchester, and even Freddie. There were people from upstate and she thought she recognized some people from Washington. All these people coming together so early in the morning. The news had spread fast. Diane watched as the tape ended. It was a good cut, she thought, a very good cut. It showed the story loud and clear. She was both proud of it and hoped it was her last cut. Everyone in the room was abuzz and excited. Many of the people congratulated her, including Henry and Ms. Winchester. Kurt and Juliana were center stage. Everyone was asking them questions about the investigation and the surveillance tapes, with Kurt answering all their questions.

"The news said that the IRS team captured the Rossi Brothers, but according to the tape you didn't capture them, did you?"

"No, we didn't capture them like grab them," Kurt explained, "we just captured them on tape."

"They're not in custody?" Miss Winchester asked.

"No, not as I understand," Diana explained. "I'm sure they will be soon though." Everyone seemed quite excited about the details.

"Well, everyone is excited!" Henry explained, "this is big, this is big for our department, you did good, really good."

"Thank you," she replied, "remember I had help from above."

Ms. Winchester assumed she meant God.

"I'm planning on taking the rest of the week off." She explained that Kurt and Juliana will probably want a vacation too.

"Vacation, work, vacation, do you want!" Ms. Winchester said, "I'll take care of the paperwork."

"Oh, thank you," Diane said, "you're always too nice to me." She waved to Kurt and Juliana, and left for home.

Joe was still asleep when she got home. She slipped back into her bed and even after he woke up, they stayed in bed all day. She only got up occasionally, to pace.

Back and forth around the bed she would walk.

"I wonder if I will get Winchester's job? I wonder if they'll promote her or find her something to do? Hell, maybe Kurt will get the job, I certainly set him up for success."

"Come back to bed, Diane, and quit worrying about it," Joe scolded her. "I'm certain your Vice President friend will call them up and force them to make you president of the whole joint." He laughed.

"You think?" she played along.

"President Diane, yes, it has a good ring to it." she laughed.

Joe replied to her fantasy, "Well, President Diane, you better just get over here close to me, because I've never made love to a President before." Diane jumped into bed and closed her eyes.

Chapter 19

A Great Idea

The rest of the week was peppered with excitement and change. The most important was that the FBI, aided by the Hope Police Department, captured and arrested the Rocci Brothers. They caught and arrested all the other workers throughout the week. Some had gone to work as usual, unaware, until they saw the police vehicles, and were caught turning around and trying to flee. The authorities gave all the credit to the IRS surveillance team, citing excellent pictures and movies, showing detailed faces and actions.

Jimbo was allowed to go back to work at the recycling plant and business boomed as people came out to donate and get a look at the crime scene. Joe visited him most of Thursday, showing off his new truck. Diane took the opportunity to visit the corporate offices and accept her new promotion.

She waved at Ms. Winchester as she went by to inspect her new office. The office was bare, devoid of any furniture at all. It did have a large plant flourishing in the corner.

"I'll keep that," she murmured to herself. As she looked the office over, planning her area and desk, she noticed all the nails and nail holes. As she examined, she noticed the small plaque. It read, Hope Country Club, Hole in One, Henry Stevens, hole #10.

"I'll keep that too," she said out loud. "Thanks, Henry, for everything."

At the store, Ronald had asked to get extra help during busy times when Joe was busy or not around. He had presented Joe with his girlfriend Patti, and although Joe disapproved, he relented. Ronald had been more than an employee; he was active and responsible for many of the improvements. Joe remembered how much he himself loved the hours when Diane joined him by working at the counter.

"She does a great Pierre!" Ronald pleaded.

On cue, Patti-Cake donned the costume, including the big bushy mustache, entered the kiosk and said, "Ma eh elp ewue?" mimicking Ronald. With that in mind, Joe allowed Ronald to hire Patti-Cake. Her real name was Patti Cacaleah Craft, but everyone called her Patti-Cake, except Joe.

Joe had also made a reservation to attend the Wine Tasting Experience again. When he surprised her with the reservations on Saturday morning, Diane started to laugh.

"Honey," she explained, "You don't go right back to the same winery for the free wine! They offer the Experience so that you will purchase their wine in the future!"

"Well, they remembered me and offered me the reservation, they seemed happy at my request," Joe told her. "Plus, I liked it! I had a great time there, last time, and want to do it again."

"I had a great time too," she answered, "and of course we can do it again. I'd be happy to go there with you today." "Well get ready," he said, "we leave in one hour." Diane quickly got ready, putting on the dress she had bought for their first meeting. I look great in that dress, she thought.

They drove to the winery in Diane's car. Joe had again put the top down as it was a beautiful day. Except for the wind messing her hair, the air was refreshing. They hurriedly joined all the waiting people and for a moment, Diane thought she recognized someone in the group but quickly realized that would be very improbable. They went off to the first stop and she realized that Joe was much more comfortable than the last time. He was smiling and whispering to people and eagerly following the tour guide. By the fifth stop, Joe was no longer whispering; he was talking aloud, and others were laughing and getting boisterous too. At the next table he loudly proclaimed, "More for everyone!" and motioned for the steward to refill everyone's glasses and, to her utter amazement, he obliged Joe and poured everyone another glass of the expensive wine. The guide seemed to encourage Joe rather than to show dismay as Diane would expect.

Finally, they went outside to the path to the vineyard. Diane hoped the fresh air would help calm his demeanor, but at the exact spot where she had fallen last time, Joe tripped and landed on the ground. Horrified, she reached down to help him but stopped. Everyone, and I mean everyone, was looking at her.

"Lie down in the grass with me!" Joe pleaded.

She looked around again, everyone was encircling her, and no one said a word. They were waiting for her!

"Lie down in the grass with me, my love!" he repeated, and she did.

They lay there just as before and again he kissed her. He then said, "Well? Will someone take our picture?"

She looked up at all the faces in the group and saw her sister Susan. Next, she saw Jimbo, then Karrie. Kurt, Juliana, Ronald and Patty Cake were there too. Everyone was taking their picture.

"What's going on?" she squeaked.

Joe rolled to his side, produced a diamond engagement ring and said, "Will you marry me, my love?"

"I do! I mean I will! Of course, I will!" she answered and hugged his neck while rolling onto then across him, kissing him frantically.

Diane jumped up triumphantly! She found Susan and hugged and kissed her, "thank you, thank you," she said over and over to all their friends that had come. Henry and Ms. Winchester were there too, everyone had showed up for the event. She turned to the group of wine-tasters and said, "You were all in on this weren't you?" and they cheered!

Everyone proceeded across the bridge to the many tables that had been set up. Joe had catered the event and the winery had donated all the wine. The entire setup was perfect and everyone was enjoying the day and the refreshments. Diane saw an emo-dressed young girl sitting next to an odd-looking young man and she pondered, Is that? I'm not even going to guess, she decided and whispered to Joe. They then went off to a nearby tree and they sat there facing each other in the shade. From a distance, it looked as if they were embracing, but as Susan approached to ask if they would like her to bring them a dish, she noticed that there was more than a foot separating them. They told her no, thank you, and that they would join everyone shortly.

"Well, what's next?" Joe quietly asked her.

Diane pondered, then moved up next to him, she put her arms around him then reached out and held his hand. As she held his hand, she slowly moved it up to their cheeks. She looked into his eyes for a long time.

Then she whispered,

A Touch of Love

"Never let go."

TWISTED TRUTH PRESS